IN THE RED ZONE

The Kelly Brothers, Book 6

by

Crista McHugh

In the Red Zone
Copyright 2015 by Crista McHugh
Edited by Gwen Hayes
Copyedited by Elizabeth MS Flynn
Cover Art by Sweet N' Spicy Designs

ISBN-13: 978-1-940559-75-9

CHAPTER ONE

"Damn!" Frank Kelly drew the word out into two syllables, a habit he'd picked up since moving to Atlanta four years ago. "Would you look at the ass on the hot thing that just walked in?"

His teammate, Treson Dyer, didn't even bother to look up from the text message he was typing out on his phone. "In a minute. It's last call for placing bets on the West Coast games."

"No, you really need to check this woman out." As it was, it was taking all the strength Frank could muster not to drool at the set of curves that had just walked into the club. He'd always been an ass man, but she took bootylicious to a whole new level. The way her dress hugged her body made him long to touch the tempting flesh covered by the thin material. She stood near the entrance, craning her neck to peer above the dancers as though she was trying to find someone.

Frank rose from his table in the VIP section and patted his friend on the chest. "On second thought, you stay right there and keep betting on basketball games. I want her all to myself."

"Have fun, Romeo," Tre replied, his gaze never leaving his phone.

Frank used the excuse of smoothing out his shirt to wipe the sweat from his palms. On the field, he was the epitome of confidence. Nothing got to him—not loud crowds, extreme weather, or the reputation of the future Hall of Fame quarterback hunched across the line from him. He just zeroed in on his target and went after it.

Women, on the other hand, were an entirely different matter. His teammates may have called him Romeo, but they never knew how tied up in knots his stomach became when he approached a woman for the first time. He hid it well behind a cocky attitude and cheeky grin, but there was still a part of him that remained a gawky teenager with fiery red hair and braces, working up the courage to ask a girl to dance.

He swallowed back his fear and slipped his trademark grin in place as he approached the woman. "Looking for me?"

Dark curls framed an angelic face and honey-colored eyes, all surrounded by flawless skin the color of coffee and cream. She arched one perfectly groomed brow. "Excuse me?"

Ouch! Her reply was almost the equivalent of a slap in the face, so he decided to change tactics. Assistance replaced arrogance, and he lowered the wattage on his charm. "You just seemed to be looking for someone, and I thought I'd be able to help."

The corner of her mouth rose into a wry smile, drawing his attention to the dark ruby color of her full lips. She was even more tempting up close.

"I know you from somewhere," she said after staring at him for what felt like an eternity. "You're Frank Kelly, aren't you?"

"The one and only." He didn't wait for permission to take her hand and tuck it into the crook of his elbow. "And I'd love to have you join me at my table."

She unwound herself from him. "Oh, no, Romeo. I've heard about you and the ladies."

Shit! Warning bells went off when she used his teammate's nickname for him.

But he continued to grin at her like she was playing right along with his plan. "Are you going to believe the rumors? Or are you tempted to find out if they're true?"

The arched brow returned, this time with a healthy dose of *Are you fucking kidding me?* attitude. But the corner of her mouth twitched, and finally, laughter bubbled out. "I'm looking for my brother, Tre. Have you seen him?"

And just like that, the proverbial bucket of ice water doused his desire. It was one thing to hit on a stranger, but his friend's sister? Even he knew better than to dig himself into that hole.

Time to change the game plan. He offered his arm to her again, this time more as a gentleman than a prospective lover. "This way, lovely lady."

She linked her arm with his and allowed him to lead her into the VIP section. Not the way he wanted to bring her back there, but it was better than getting smacked for his advances.

When they got to the table, his teammate was still furiously typing away.

The woman placed her hand on her hip. "Hey, Tre, put

that thing down for five seconds and say hello to me."

Tre jerked and blinked several times when he looked up. "Kiana, you made it." He tucked the phone into his pocket long enough to stand and give his sister a hug. "What took so long?"

She glanced over at Frank. "Romeo here was trying to make a move on me."

"Dude, you were hitting on my sister?" Tre smacked the back of Frank's head and gave him a warning glare that clearly said *hands off*.

"I didn't know." Frank rubbed the spot on his head. Tre had never even mentioned having a sister, much less that she would be joining them tonight.

He slumped back into his chair and studied the siblings. They had the same shape of eyes, both fringed by thick lashes. The same chins. The same foreheads. Enough to hint at a family resemblance, even though she had a much lighter complexion.

"Treating me like the dirty family secret again?" she asked lightheartedly and took the seat beside Tre.

"No, just busy."

Even though her brother brushed off her question, Frank was intrigued. He leaned forward. "I can't imagine how someone as lovely as you could be considered a dirty secret."

"Believe it, man," Tre snapped. "I'm her brother from another mother."

Kiana rolled her eyes. "What he means to say is that our father had a problem keeping his zipper up. I'm his half-sister."

"Enough said." Frank's spidey senses told him that was

one topic they didn't need to continue.

"But I still love you, Kiki." Tre placed a kiss on Kiana's cheek and went back to his phone.

An awkward silence followed that made Frank squirm in his seat. Tre obviously was more interested in watching basketball scores roll in and estimating his winnings for the night than hanging out with his sister. But if Frank dared to ask her out on the dance floor, he might open himself up to more than just a warning glance from his friend. A wise man might have found some excuse to leave the table, but Frank had never been accused of being wise.

Especially when it came to women.

An older song from Pitbull blasted through the speakers of the club, and Frank rose from his seat and approached Kiana. "Care to dance?"

A flicker of amusement shone from her golden-brown eyes. "Depends."

"On what?"

"On how well you can dance." She raked her gaze over him, her expression one of challenge.

Frank chuckled and rolled his hips in time to the Latin rhythm. "I've got plenty of moves."

More laughter rose from that tempting mouth, and his chest tightened. He didn't dare breathe until she held out her hand.

"Not bad for a white boy," she teased.

"You might find I'm full of surprises." He took her hand and cast one more glance at her brother to make sure it was safe to take her out. When Tre didn't look up, he led her to the packed dance floor.

The music throbbed through the sound system, and flashing lights illuminated the sea of writhing bodies with shadows that concealed faces and highlighted sexy silhouettes. Once they were deep enough into the crowd, Frank grew brave enough to rest his hands on the curve of her hips. She danced along with the beat, each sensuous sway of her body heightening the fire flowing through his veins. He followed her lead and lowered his mouth to her ear, singing some of the lyrics of the song.

"I know you want me. You know I want you."

Her grin widened. "You can dance, but you can't sing."

And another blow to his pride. At least this time, she softened it by wrapping her arms around his neck and pulling him closer her.

He dropped his hands to the top of that luscious ass that had called to him the moment he'd first spotted her. Now it was his turn to take the lead. Once again, he found himself thanking his mother for insisting he take ballroom dance classes when he was in junior high. The experience revived the salsa moves like an old memory. He pressed her against him and guided her movements, watching for any sign that he'd overstepped his bounds. Instead, he was rewarded with heavily hooded eyes and a seductive smile that made his dick ache with desire.

They don't call me "Romeo" for nothing.

And he wanted her. Badly.

Too bad she was Tre's sister. If she weren't, he'd be all too ready to invite her back to his place after a few more songs.

The song faded into the next one, but she didn't move away from him. Instead, she coyly met his gaze and ran her fingers up and down his neck.

He found himself staring at her lips, longing to taste them. Sweat prickled along his spine. He tried to divert his attention to the music, the lights, the people around him, but he kept coming back to the siren in his arms. So tempting, and yet so dangerous. And he knew if he gave into her, he'd be lost.

He was spared from falling into her snare when she stiffened in his arms.

"Shit," she hissed under her breath, staring at something behind him. "Let's get out of here."

"What's wrong?"

"Don't ask." She took his hand and pulled him toward the VIP section.

He'd managed to take one step before a hand clamped on his shoulder and spun him around. His hand reflexively curled into a fist, but he'd had enough run-ins with the law not to swing blindly.

A black man a few inches shorter than him stood less than a foot away, surrounded by an entourage of his buddies. The expression on his face spoke of pure trouble, and Frank started calculating his odds if he took him on.

"Kiana," the man said with a subtle lift of his chin. "I thought that was you."

"Fuck off, Malcolm." She tugged at Frank's hand, but a member of Malcolm's party cut off her escape route.

"Ah, is that any way to say hello to me, Boo? How's my baby girl?" Malcolm reached for her arm, but she shrugged out of his way and moved closer to Frank.

The mixture of both irritation and fear on her face kicked Frank's protective urges into overdrive. He moved between Kiana and their unwelcome visitor. "I don't think she wants you around."

Malcolm replied with a dismissive snort. "And who are you, whitey?"

"The man she was dancing with until you decided to interrupt us." Frank kept his words low and even, sticking to that line from Hamlet. *Beware of entrance to a quarrel, but being in, Bear't that the opposed may beware of thee.* He didn't want trouble, but if the guy didn't take a hint soon, he wouldn't back down from defending Kiana.

Malcolm's eyes widened ever so slightly before he laughed it off, his whole body relaxed in comparison to the increasing tension in the rest of his entourage. "I always knew you were more white than black," he tossed out at Kiana.

She winced, and Frank's fingers dug into his palms. What he wouldn't give to punch that smirk off Malcolm's face.

He took a step toward Malcolm, drawing up every bit of his six foot three, two hundred and fifty pound frame. "I'll say it simply enough for you to grasp. Leave her alone."

"Or you'll what?"

His pulse throbbed through his temples. After getting caught in a compromising position with one of Jenny's cousins after the engagement ceremony in Seattle a few weeks ago, he'd promised Adam he'd behave, that he'd stay out of trouble. But right now, all he wanted to do was shut that arrogant punk up with his fist. He glared down at Malcolm, waiting for the smaller man to cower. Instead, the expression on the man's face dared him to bring it on.

A sharp cry jerked his attention away from the staring match. One of Malcolm's friends had Kiana by the shoulder and was murmuring a string of lewd comments while he ground his body against her.

Frank's vision clouded red and he swung.

Chapter Two

Kiana's breath caught as Frank punched at the asshole who'd been trying to feel her up. She'd barely had to time to free herself from his grip before Frank's fist connected with the guy's nose with a sickening crunch. Blood splattered her face and dress, and a squeal of disgust mingled with fear escaped from her lips. She added a few more feet of distance between her and the two men exchanging blows, but like much of the crowd gathering around them, she couldn't turn away.

The night had started out so well. For the first time in ages, she felt sexy, confident, alive. And the more attention Frank gave her, the stronger those emotions became. Dancing in his arms reminded her of those carefree days in college where she could flirt with the best of them and not worry about the consequences when one thing led to another. If Malcolm hadn't interrupted them, she might have let her guard down enough to indulge in a kiss or two.

But that was all she would've allowed Frank Kelly. She

knew better than to play with a player. She'd come to the club with only one objective, and that was to secure a celebrity endorsement from Frank Kelly for her foundation. She was willing to go to any length to get it, even if it meant playing along with his flirtations. But her plan went to hell the second Malcolm entered the picture.

The last player who'd burned her stood a few yards away, encouraging his buddies to jump into the fight and beat the crap out of Frank, but not making a move to dirty his own hands in the brawl. He only hit those he considered weaker than him. Thankfully, his entourage saw the beating their friend was receiving and hesitated to become the next person to feel the fury of Frank's fists.

When he saw none of them were willing to do his dirty work, Malcolm reached into his jacket, and her heart stuttered to a stop. She knew the pissed-off glint in his eye well enough, as well as his habit of carrying a concealed weapon. As far as she knew, he'd never fired the .44 he liked to hide in his clothes. It was more for intimidation, for street cred, than anything else. But the rage twisting his face signaled he might have reached the point where he wanted to pull the trigger. And just like the night he'd pointed it at her, she couldn't tell if it was loaded.

The dull black grip of a handgun appeared from under Malcolm's jacket. Her ex's gaze never wavered from the man who'd challenged him. The man who continued to pummel his lackey. The man whose back was to him.

Something snapped inside of Kiana. If she didn't do something, Frank would be shot, and it would be all her fault. And then, who was to say that she wouldn't be next? This time, she refused to huddle in a corner and beg for mercy. This time, she would take control of the situation and act. She darted forward as Malcolm pulled out his gun. Her hand connected with the side of his arm as he extended it. She snapped it up as he squeezed the trigger.

The deafening shot rang in her ears long after the bullet left the chamber. A strobe light above them exploded. Showers of sparks and shards of glass rained down on the crowd. Then pandemonium erupted.

Screams filled the club, and the occupants ran toward the doors. Frank stopped punching his opponent long enough to get up on his knees and spy Malcolm, still holding the gun.

"You stupid bitch!" Malcolm shouted, his free hand connecting with her cheek.

The familiar taste of blood filled her mouth, and she tumbled to the floor.

A feral growl rose behind her, and she lifted her head just in time to see Frank tackle Malcolm as though they were on the football field. Her ex's eyes bulged when Frank's shoulder connected with his gut. A grunt of pain escaped his lips. The clang of metal followed, and Malcolm's handgun slid off in the dark shadows of the dance floor.

"You need to learn some manners," Frank said before delivering a solid punch to Malcolm's jaw.

Kiana bit her swollen lip, fighting back the urge to cheer Frank on. For the last two years, she'd wanted to see Malcolm get what was coming to him. She wanted him to feel the pain and humiliation of being hit by someone bigger than him. She wanted him to experience what she'd endured during their stormy relationship. And now Frank was dishing it up for her.

A hand clamped down on her shoulder, and Tre yanked her to her feet. "Let's get out of here before the cops arrive."

"But what about Frank?" She nodded toward the red-haired man who was exacting the punishment she'd always wanted to give Malcolm.

"He's on his own." Tre dragged her to the back door as the police were pouring in through the front doors. "Better him than us."

She was halfway to her car before she managed to dig her heels in and stop her brother. "I'm not going to let him take the blame."

"Will you use your head for a goddamned minute, woman?" Tre pulled a handkerchief out of his pocket and pressed it against her busted bottom lip. "You could've gotten killed in there."

"We would've been fine if Malcolm had just stuck to his restraining order."

"All the more reason to get out of there."

"But we did nothing wrong." She pushed her brother away. "And Frank was the one who almost got killed trying to protect me."

"Frank's been known to be stupid like that. Now come on." Tre grabbed her arm and continued to pull her toward her car. Once they got to it, he opened the door and pushed her into the driver's seat. "Go straight home."

"But what about Frank?"

"He can handle himself." Her brother glanced around, the blue lights from the police cars casting eerie shadows on the worried lines of his face. "Get out of here before someone from Malcolm's gang comes looking for you."

"But—"

"For fuck's sake, Kiana, think of Savannah."

A shock of fear raced down her spine and locked her muscles. She closed her eyes and shifted her priorities. Tre was right. She needed to go home, not risk her life any more tonight. There were more important things in life. She nodded and inserted her key in the ignition.

"I'll check on you later." Tre pressed the lock button before he closed her door and stepped away.

She started her car and pulled out into the street, her hands beginning to shake from what just happened. Her breath came and went in the same unsteady, quick tempo, and the side of her face throbbed. Tears stung her eyes. But she managed to round the corner to get on the main road in front of the club.

She stopped and watched the police lead a handcuffed Frank out of the club and into the back seat of a cruiser.

A new wave of guilt assaulted her and chased away the fear. She'd been a victim once, but never again. She could take action. And she could make sure Frank didn't have to take the fall. Perhaps, if luck was on her side, she might even be able to get what she'd come to the club for in the process.

She waited until she had driven several blocks away before she pulled over on the side of the road and pulled out her cell phone. A few rings later, a sleepy voice answered.

"Tasha, it's Kiana. Sorry to bother you at this time of night, but I have a huge favor to ask of you."

***

14

Frank sat in the jail cell and pressed the cold pack against his swollen eye.

How the hell am I going to explain this one to Adam?

It had been almost two years since he'd last been in this predicament. Two years since he'd lost his temper and let his fists get the better of him. Two years since he'd beaten the crap out of someone and ended up in jail. He'd thought he'd mastered his anger issues, but the moment he saw that guy feeling up Kiana, he'd lost it.

Only now, he was starting to realize how close he'd come to losing his life.

He'd heard the gun before he'd seen it, and he could only guess that Kiana was the one who'd kept him from getting a bullet in the back. She was the one pushing Malcolm's arm up into the air when he'd turned around. That is, until the bastard hit her.

Frank's hand curled into a fist. There was never any excuse for hitting a woman. Ever. And he only wished the police had let him finish beating the crap out of that asshole before they'd arrested him.

His thoughts turned to her. He'd lost track of Kiana once he'd head-butted Malcolm's gut. He could only hope she was okay. Maybe instead of using his one phone call to ask Adam to bail him out, he'd call Tre and make sure she was safe.

The cold pack was losing its chill, and he lowered it to test his eye. A narrow slit of light came through the swollen eyelid, but the images were too hazy to make it useful.

At least it was the off season. He didn't need perfect vision until the fall.

He leaned back against the cold cinder block wall and winced. He was going to be sorer tomorrow than he was after a division rivalry game. But as he remembered the way Kiana felt in his arms, he grinned.

Yeah, she'd been totally worth it.

A low buzz came from down the hallway, and footsteps came closer. The door to his cell opened. "Come with me, Kelly," the guard ordered.

Time to make that phone call.

But instead of leading him to the phone, the guard led him to another guard holding his belongings. "Make sure you have everything."

A hint of unease crawled up his spine. He'd been arrested enough times to know this wasn't protocol. "Um, have I been bailed out already?"

"Something like that," the guard replied.

Frank made a quick inventory of his things. Watch. Wallet. Phone. Valet parking stub. It was all there, and he didn't intend to linger in the Fulton County jail any longer than necessary. He nodded to the guard and was escorted out.

He stopped short when he spotted a familiar set of curves waiting for him.

"I'll take him from here," Kiana said in a tone that permitted no arguments. "Let's go, Frank."

"You bailed me out?" he asked.

Her eyes darted around the room, and the set of her shoulders hardened. "I'll tell you more in the car."

In other words, he was to keep his mouth shut until then.

He followed her to the parking garage and waited for

her to unlock a late-model gold Lexus ES. She climbed into the driver's seat in silence and started the car. Once he'd crammed himself into the passenger seat, she threw the car in reverse and backed out of the parking spot before he could buckle his seatbelt. "Keep your head down."

He was about to ask her why, until he spotted the media vans waiting in front of the jail. A curse flew from his lips, and he reclined the seat until he was lying in the backseat. He waited for the camera flashes or the spotlights, but Kiana managed to drive past them without inciting the frenzy that had followed him the last time he'd been bailed out.

Once they were safely out of sight, he sat back up. "Thanks."

She nodded, her cheek starting to show signs of a bruise.

The anger revived in his gut. "Who was that asshole?"

"An ex," she replied, her two-word reply revealing a hint of caution.

"Where is he now?" Every time he saw that bruise, he wanted to finish what he started.

"Don't know, and don't care." A tremor filled her voice, and she gripped the steering wheel. She swallowed hard, and when she spoke again, the fear was gone. "I wanted to thank you for coming to my aid back there."

"Anything for a beautiful lady."

The corner of her mouth rose into a wry smile. "Are you always this much of a flirt?"

"Nope." He laced his fingers behind his neck and leaned back. "Sometimes I'm worse."

That earned him a small chuckle, and his chest tightened. He liked hearing her laugh, especially after tonight's events.

"So how much do I owe you for my bail?"

"Nothing." The smile faded, and the nervous twitch in her hands returned.

"Nonsense. I know how much they charged last time—"

"There was no bail because there were no charges filed against you."

He snapped his head up. "Excuse me?"

She wiggled in her seat and turned to get on the Downtown Connector. "I made a few phone calls and got them to drop the charges against you."

"How did you manage that? And furthermore, how much did it cost?"

"Nothing." She turned to give him a sheepish smile. "Once I explained the situation to a few people, I was able to get the assault charges dropped in exchange for a small favor."

He let out a low whistle. "You must know some people in high places."

"Something like that," she said with a shrug. "So where's your place? Sandy Springs?"

"Roswell." He gave her his address, still giving her a side eye. "Although I'll warn you, I'm a bit too sore to live up to my reputation tonight, if that's what you're looking for."

She laughed again, and his heart gave an unsteady thump. God, he loved that low, rich sound.

"I doubt you're in any condition to drive yourself home

tonight, so I'm just playing taxi service."

"But maybe when I've recovered…"

She laughed even harder and merged onto Georgia-400. "You don't know how to let up, do you?"

He gave her his cheeky grin, ignoring the pain around his swollen eye. "Nope. I figured you had to have a reason to bail me out of the slammer."

The laughter vanished, and she bit that swollen bottom lip. "Actually, there was a reason I got those charges dropped."

And it had nothing to do with her wanting to ride him senseless in the bedroom, judging by the way her shoulders tightened again. "I'm listening."

"Well, first off, I wanted to apologize for tonight. If you hadn't been dancing with me, you'd never have gotten into that fight, and I don't know what I would've done if you'd gotten shot."

"Aw," he drawled, placing his hand over his heart. "So you do care about me?"

She rolled her eyes and shook her head. "You are something else."

"It's all part of my Irish charm." He grew serious, though, and added, "But I take it there's another reason why you used your connections to get me out."

"Um, actually, there is." She twisted her palms around the steering wheel a couple of times. "You know who my dad was, right?"

"Who doesn't? Marshall Dyer was a legend. I remember attending one of his linebacker camps as a kid and being in complete awe of him."

She nodded and waited a moment before continuing.

"Just before he passed away last year, he started up a foundation to provide proper gear for youth football programs. He suffered multiple concussions during his career, and he wanted to make sure no kid suffered the after-effects like he did. I took over for him, and, well…" She drew up into a full-body wince, her brows forming a wrinkle above her nose. "I haven't been able to generate the interest I'd like for the organization."

"And where do I fit into this?"

"We're having a fundraiser in a couple of months, and I'd really appreciate it if you could give it a celebrity endorsement."

He drew in a slow breath, mulling over her request. "What about Tre?"

"We both know Tre's a third stringer and in danger of getting cut any day now." Her words were blunt but honest, without any traces of bitterness or anger. "You're a Pro-Bowler, a big man in the football community. People know your name as well as they knew my father's. And if your name became associated with the foundation or even with me—"

"Where do you come into this scheme?"

She squirmed under his scrutiny. "I'll be upfront with you, Frank, and tell you that I'm not interested in a relationship or anything close to that right now. However, I wouldn't be opposed to a few staged dates until the gala."

"A fake relationship?"

She licked her lips and nodded. "If you and I show up at a couple of events or restaurants around town, people will think we're dating, and when they look me up, they'll find their way to the foundation."

"And how realistic are you willing to make these fake dates look? Would you spare a kiss or two for the camera?"

"If necessary. I know I'm not like some of the other girls you've dated, but I'm respectable, and my squeaky clean image will help yours by association. I'll play my part if it helps the foundation, but I didn't want to lead you on in thinking it was anything real or that I'd be hopping into the sack with you on the first date. I'm not that type of girl."

She was so upfront, so honest about her commitment to her father's foundation, part of him was ready to agree right there. But a little voice in the back of his mind urged caution. It sounded good in general, but he needed to dig a little deeper before he associated his name with anything. Not to mention the fact he wanted more than just a few staged kisses from her. "I'll need to speak with my agent first."

"I understand." She took the Roswell exit and slowed the car down to comply with the speed limit. "All our information is on the website, and I'm willing to answer any questions you or your agent may have. I just—"

He waited for her to continue, but when she didn't, he asked, "Just what?"

"I just don't want the foundation to fail. Daddy was so passionate about it, and I feel like I'd be letting him down if I couldn't carry on his work. I'm a very private person, but I'm willing to go out of my comfort zone if it will make this fundraiser a success."

Once again, she became the damsel in distress, and he

was unable to resist her call for help. "I'll see what I can do."

She rewarded him with a smile that radiated pure joy. "Thank you."

An odd feeling tugged at his gut when he saw it. Yeah, she knew how to press all his buttons. Too bad she was forbidden fruit.

He waved to the security guard at the entrance to his gated community. Thankfully, his celebrity status made him easily recognizable. Well, that and his red hair. The guard let them pass, and before he knew it, Kiana was pulling into his driveway.

"You going to be okay?" he asked. "You're welcome to crash here if you need to hide out someplace safe."

She shook her head. "Thanks, but I'm pretty safe at my place."

The familiar awkwardness took over as he got out of the car. He wanted to see her again, but he wasn't sure if she only wanted him for her foundation. "I'll be in touch with you in a few days."

"Sounds good." Her chin quivered, despite the brave face she was trying to give him. She'd been shaken up tonight.

"Are you sure you'll be all right tonight?" he asked one more time, the car door still open.

"Yeah, I'll be fine." The quivering vanished. "Thanks again, Frank, for everything."

A warm glow filled her honey-colored eyes, and he wondered if "everything" included what had passed between them on the dance floor before they'd been interrupted.

"You are most welcome, lovely lady." He closed the door and watched her drive away with a sense of uncertainty.

One thing was certain, though. He would see Kiana Dyer again.

And hopefully, soon.

CHAPTER THREE

Frank stared at his reflection and cursed. It was bad enough he'd been the only one of his brothers cursed with red hair. Now he had a fist-sized shiner around his left eye to add to his odd look. At least the swelling had gone down from last night. He could only imagine what Kiana must've thought of him when she drove him home last night. No wonder she'd turned down his invitation.

He shuffled to the shower and scrubbed away the remnants of the club—the smoke, the booze, the blood. The only thing he didn't want to forget was how tempting the goddess in his arms felt as their bodies moved together. They would've made magic in the sack—no doubt there. But she also spelled trouble.

Too bad he liked trouble.

Once he dried off and got dressed, he found his phone and called Adam.

His eldest brother answered with, "What have you gotten yourself into now?"

"Nothing."

"You only call when you need me to bail you out," Adam accused.

Frank's cheeks burned, and he scratched the back of his head. "Yeah, I guess I haven't been a very good brother lately."

"So?"

"Let me start off by saying I'm not in jail."

"For once."

Embarrassment turned to irritation, but it still heated his skin. "Hey, I've been good lately. It's been two years since I got into trouble."

"But there's something you want to talk about, judging by the guilt in your voice and the fact you're calling me at nine in the morning on a Sunday."

Damn, his brother knew him too well. "Well, they say confession is good for the soul."

"You'll need more than just ten Hail Marys to absolve you of some of your sins, especially after that incident involving you and Jenny's cousin last month. I don't think the Nguyen family will ever forgive you for that."

"It was all her idea to hook up in the laundry room, and I wasn't going to turn down a little hottie like her."

"And of course, you were nothing more than a victim." A lighter, teasing note filled Adam's voice. "So tell me what happened."

"I'm sure it made the news."

Now it was Adam's turn to curse. The sound of a keyboard clicking filled the background. A minute later, more cursing followed. "Please tell me you weren't in that nightclub shooting."

"Bingo."

Panic rose into his brother's voice. "Shit, you're not in the hospital or anything?"

Frank toyed with the idea of stringing Adam along, but the panic seemed too real. "I'm fine. Just sporting a lovely black eye from it all."

A string of incomprehensible muttering filled the line for a good twenty seconds. "Start from the beginning, and by that, I don't mean you were in the club, minding your own business."

"But I was," Frank said innocently. "I was hanging out with Tre when his sister, Kiana, joined us. We started dancing, then her ex showed up, gave us some grief, and one thing led to another."

"Jesus, Frank, are you a magnet for trouble?" Adam paused. "It says here that two people were sent to the hospital."

"I didn't hit them that hard." But part of him was glad to learn those creeps needed medical attention. Hopefully, they'd learn not to mess with Kiana again.

"Frank." His brother said his name like a plea to behave. "According to the article, one of them was the gunman."

"That would be Kiana's ex."

"Shit! You got into a fight with a man with a gun? What kind of hot-headed idiot are you?"

Frank collapsed on his oversize couch and stared at the ceiling. "He tried to pull the gun out mid-fight, but Kiana knocked it out of his hand."

"So the woman was involved in the fight, too? That's a first for you."

He grinned. Maybe Kiana wasn't a complete damsel in

distress. She'd had his back when it counted. "Listen, the fight itself doesn't matter. I'm safe, and the good news is, Kiana managed to get the charges dropped."

Another pause answered him. "And you somehow managed to stay out of the media this time."

That was a first. He'd been booked, which meant any of the scumbags trolling the jail's records would've been able to find his name. Maybe her connections were more extensive than he first thought.

"But the gunman was some kind of celebrity. A rapper called King Mal."

Frank snorted. That prick *would* call himself King Mal. "And he'll be the one facing charges, not me."

"Looks like it." A squeak came from the background, and Frank imagined Adam leaning back in his desk chair. "So, is that the only reason you called? To brag about putting two men in the hospital without getting arrested?"

"More like reassure you that I'm fine. I know how you worry."

"I'm going to be as gray as Dad was before I'm forty."

"And you and Lia don't even have kids yet."

"That's because I'm too busy trying to take care of all my little brothers." A wistful note filled Adam's voice. Frank knew his eldest brother and his wife wanted kids. If Adam had his way, he'd have a brood as large as their parents had. "What else did you want to tell me?"

"Kiana asked if I'd be willing to give an endorsement for the foundation she runs, and I wanted to do a little digging before I agree to it."

"Want me to have Cully do some snooping?" Adam replied, dropping the name of the private investigator his business had used on more than one occasion.

"Not that extreme. More like I want your opinion. It's the Marshall Dyer Foundation."

A few more clicks of the keyboard. "Looks legit. And I remember how you idolized Dyer when you were a kid."

"Yeah."

The way he drawled out the word must've revealed his hesitations because Adam asked, "So what's the holdup?"

"The woman in charge."

"Expecting more gun fights?"

"More like wondering how I'll be able to remain professional around her. She seems to think staging a fake relationship between us will help draw attention to the foundation, but I don't want to cross the line. And I know I'll be tempted to when I'm near her."

Adam chuckled. "Thinking of the consequences before you act for once. I'm impressed. And I'm looking at her picture right now. Not bad."

"Not bad?" Frank sat up. "Are you blind? She's gorgeous."

"Sorry, but my tastes tend toward petite Italian women," Adam replied with more light-hearted laughter.

"You see my dilemma, though, right? Plus, she's Tre's sister, and I already got the *don't go there* vibe from him."

"But…?"

Frank slouched back against the sofa again and ran his finger through his short hair. "But I'm stuck trying to decide if I want to risk working that close to her."

"You left out one important detail."

"What's that?"

"What kind of signals are you getting from her?"

"No fucking clue." The frustration in his voice matched what he'd felt last night when she'd turned down his invitation to stay with him. He'd seen enough to know she'd be a hard one to win over, but worth it. "Mixed signals at best. I mean, it was her idea to play the part of my fake girlfriend, so she can't find me that repulsive."

"Hmm." He could almost picture Adam rubbing his chin in thought. "Why does she want to pursue a fake relationship?"

"She thinks it will draw more attention to the foundation. And she mentioned that being seen with someone like her might help clean up my image, as well."

"True, but there might be a way to work this in your favor."

Frank grinned. He knew his big brother would come through. "I'm all ears."

CHAPTER FOUR

Kiana stared at the mockups on her computer screen. They were for an ad that would run in the *Atlanta Journal Constitution* this Sunday announcing the gala and silent auction fundraiser for the foundation, but all her attempts seemed to fall short of what she needed, and they were due this afternoon.

She pressed her fingers against her temples. What little funds she had were dedicated to the event and paying her lone staff member until then. She couldn't afford to hire some swanky PR firm to handle this for her. Hell, she'd be lucky to break even, based on the meager number of tickets they'd sold. She needed to get the media's attention, and she'd hoped Frank would've agreed to help her, but so far, almost a week had passed without a word from him or his representative.

She was almost tempted to ask Tre to give Frank a nudge, but the possible repercussions held her back. First off, Tre would be pissed she wasn't asking for his endorsement. Their relationship had been strained, at best, since she'd moved in with their dad more than fifteen years ago. Despite his seemingly loving words, she'd always caught a hint of resentment from him. The tension only worsened after their father had died and she'd received a sizable inheritance.

Second, she'd seen the silent warning her brother had given Frank. As if she needed her little brother to intervene in her nonexistent love life. She'd walked on the wild side, but she'd learned her lesson far too well.

Don't play with a player.

And Frank Kelly was every inch a player. The man oozed both sex and charm. If she hadn't already been aware of his reputation, he probably would've gotten her out of her panties before the night was done. As it was, it had been hard enough to turn down his invitation to stay at his place Saturday night. She'd seen what the man could do with his hips on the dance floor, and she could only imagine what he was capable of doing in the bedroom.

Watch it, girl. You know what kind of trouble men like him can be.

Especially men who knew how to hit.

So why on earth had she been crazy enough to propose that whole fake relationship thing? It was just asking for trouble. But she'd been desperate and decided to use his attraction to her to her advantage and entice him to her cause. The more time she spent with him, the more she'd be able to sell him on endorsing her foundation. At least she'd been upfront from the start that it wouldn't go anywhere.

She massaged her temples, taking care not to press too hard on her right side. The swelling had disappeared from her cheek, but the tenderness still lingered. Thankfully, she'd already had enough practice covering bruises with makeup.

A knock sounded at her door, and her assistant, Sherita, poked her head in. "Kiana, Frank Kelly is here to see you."

Her stomach twisted, and her pulse kicked into overdrive. "He is?"

Sherita nodded, a knowing grin appearing on her lips.

Kiana stared at the disarray in her desk and made a mad attempt to organize it. Then she ran her hands over her hair. "How do I look?"

Her assistant came in and closed the door behind her. "Flustered."

She leaned back in her desk chair. "Not good."

"But perfectly understandable." Sherita fanned herself and acted like she was blowing out a flame.

Yeah, Frank Kelly was hot, and she wasn't the only one who thought so.

Kiana laughed, the tension easing from her shoulders. "Let him in."

"Are you sure? 'Cause I don't mind the view from my desk."

She continued to laugh, but nodded. "Yeah, but how much work do you think you'd get done with him standing there?"

"None." Sherita grinned but stepped back out to fetch Frank.

Kiana used those final seconds to check her reflection in the hand mirror she kept in her desk drawer. Not perfect, but at least she didn't have any lipstick on her teeth.

Her gaze fell on the framed picture of her daughter on the corner of her desk as the door opened. She snatched it and tucked it into the drawer along with her mirror. She'd managed to keep her out of the spotlight since her birth and she intended to keep it that way.

Frank ambled into her office, and her breath hitched. She'd thought he'd been sexy in the club, but today took it to a whole other level. *Hot* didn't begin to describe him. The gray Notre Dame T-shirt clung to the well-defined muscles of his upper arms and broad chest, while his jeans molded his ass in a way that practically begged her to squeeze it.

"Hey there, lovely lady," he greeted with a wink and grin.

His flirtatious behavior broke her awe, and she found her voice. "What took you so long?"

"I had to make sure I was beautiful enough to grace your presence, especially if you had posing for pictures in mind." He touched the eye that had been swollen shut Saturday night. Only a faint yellow tinge remained of the bruise.

More like he was playing mind games with her. Men were like that. It was no different when they asked for her number and then waited a week to call. At least she knew where she stood with him.

She pushed back from her desk and crossed her legs, noting the way his gaze fell to them. Silent laughter filled her mind. He could play mind games, but she still had the upper hand.

"So, what's the verdict?" she asked.

"I'm in." He sat in the chair across from her, his massive build making the chair appear smaller than it was, and crossed his arms. "But once I commit to something, I'm not content unless I'm giving it a hundred and ten percent. And I have a few ideas that may give the foundation even more exposure."

"Such as?"

"Let's start with lunch."

Her pulse kicked up a notch. "Lunch?"

He nodded, his grin widening. "It is noon, in case you failed to notice."

The grumbling in her stomach answered. "I suppose we could discuss this over lunch."

"Perfect." He bounced up from the chair like a kid hearing the recess bell. "I took the liberty of making reservations down the street. You up for a walk?"

"How far?" She glanced down at her heels and wondered if they'd be up to the challenge.

He named a restaurant a block away.

Her mouth watered. One of her favorite places to eat in Atlanta. "I'm there."

She grabbed her purse and waved to Sherita on the way out of the small office she rented in Midtown. Maybe once the foundation got bigger, they could afford more room and a larger staff, but at the moment, it was a two-woman show.

Frank's hand fell to the small of her back as they got on the elevator, and a shiver coursed through her. His hand was warm, but possessive. And although her body welcomed his touch, her mind urged caution.

Focus on business. "So, what did you want to discuss over

lunch?" she asked, keeping her voice light.

"A surefire way to make sure everyone knows about your father's foundation."

Something about the twinkle in his blue eyes made her stomach flip. "Do you ever stop flirting?"

"Sorry, but it's as natural as breathing to me."

Uh-huh. And all the more reason why she should stay away. Of course, it didn't help that the close proximity allowed her to catch a whiff of his spicy cologne. It was clean, yet masculine. Something she could enjoy breathing in all night as they wrestled under the covers.

The elevator opened on the ground floor, and she darted out, anxious to get a few feet between them.

He caught up to her with a few easy strides. "Do I need to spoil the fun by acting serious for once?"

"That would be helpful." *Both for me and my sanity.*

"Anything to help a woman as lovely as yourself."

She found herself laughing. Maybe he couldn't stop flirting.

His teasing grin widened. "Laughter always eases the tension." His face grew a tad more solemn as he added, "So it's just you and Sherita running things?"

She nodded. "I'm hoping the fundraiser will allow us to hire more staff, but she's all I can afford at the moment. As it stands now, we're already overwhelmed. School budgets keep getting cut, and requests to replace wornout pads and helmets keep piling up."

"The kids deserve better."

"Damn right they do." For a moment, she forgot about the sexy man beside her and got lost in what had become her mission. "All this evidence is coming out about the long-term effects of concussions in athletes, yet they can't even give a peewee player a proper helmet. And don't even get me started about the sorry-ass equipment we've seen at some of the local high schools. Those guys hit hard, and we've been seeing an alarming rise in injuries, especially at some of the inner city schools that lack the Roswell budgets."

She paused to catch her breath and look up at Frank. Gone was the cheeky flirt. In his place stood a genuinely engaged man who watched her with something akin to admiration in his eyes.

"You're very passionate about this, aren't you?" he asked softly.

She nodded, her throat choking up from a memory. "Just like my daddy was."

"Then I'll do all I can to help." He tucked one of her flyaway curls behind her ear.

His touch was so light, so gentle, so unexpected from the man who'd sent Malcolm to the hospital with his fists. Again, her mind urged caution, warring with the warmth stirring in her veins. Experience had taught her to avoid men who were the dangerous combination of charming and violent.

She took a step back and resumed walking toward the restaurant. "What's this surefire way to gain some attention for the foundation?"

"Establishing a subtle connection *before* I make the official endorsement."

"Oh?" The spark of intelligence behind his words intrigued her. Maybe there was more to him than just the stereotypical dumb jock.

"You and I appear in public together starting right now to make people wonder if we're dating. Share a few meals, a few kisses, maybe hint at a private sleepover. Then, after a couple of weeks, I'll gladly plaster my name and likeness on anything you need."

For the second time in less than a block, she halted. "And you think that's going to work like that?"

He wrapped his arm around her waist and urged her along. "It was your idea, not mine. No time like the present. After all, those kids need proper equipment."

Of course he'd use the kids as leverage. "But to be clear, we're not dating."

His bottom lip jutted out into a smoldering pout that captivated her, distracting her and allowing him to wrap his other arm around her waist and pull her closer. "Are you sure I can't convince you to reconsider?"

For a brief second, she allowed herself to indulge in the warmth of his embrace, in the sparks of desire that flared between them. It was the dance floor all over again. Her voice cracked in a final plea that belied her crumbling resistance. "Frank..."

"Fine," he said, brushing his lips against her forehead in a feather-light kiss before he let her go. "I'll behave."

She released the breath she never realized she'd been holding. The man was proving to be more seductive than she'd first imagined.

He opened the door to the restaurant and gave his name to the hostess. A minute later, they were being shown to their table with a crowd of gazes following them. But then, what should she expect when she was in the presence of someone like Frank Kelly? If his size and bright red hair didn't attract attention, then his sheer charisma did. The man lit up a room as much as he electrified the football field. People noticed him.

Maybe her idea of the two of them appearing in public had some merit after all. She never got this much attention when she entered a room by herself.

He chose the seat beside her instead of sitting across from her. Once the server took their orders, he leaned in toward her. "So, now that you know you have my unwavering support, what do you say we enjoy getting to know each other?"

"You mean like on a date?"

"Did I call it that?" he asked in mock innocence.

She rolled her eyes with a smile. She had to give him points for persistence.

"Remember, this was all your idea." He took a long drink of sweet tea. "Are you older or younger than Tre?"

"Eight months older." She fed off his carefree air and added, "You could say we're Irish twins."

His grin widened. "I've got one of those myself. There's eleven months between me and Gideon. I think my parents raised the white flag after that."

"If I was your mama, I would've raised the white flag after you."

"Yeah, I kind of broke the mold. I'm sure if she had to do it again, she'd just have me and none of my other brothers."

He was so full of himself, yet in a self-deprecating way. She liked the mixture of confidence tempered with a hint of humility and found herself drawn to him even more. "Are you saying you're her favorite?"

"Is there any doubt?"

The playful banter continued throughout the meal as he shared stories about his childhood. After they ordered dessert, he grew silent and studied her with his head tilted slightly. "Forgive me if I'm treading on something you don't want to talk about, but what's the story with you and Tre?"

Her back tightened. He'd been so open and cheerful about his family that she envied him. Her family was filled with enough drama and secrets to warrant a reality TV show. "What do you mean?"

"Well, for starters, he never mentioned you before Saturday night."

"I told you. Our father had some trouble keeping his zipper up. He had a fling with my mom while he was married to Tre's mom."

Frank nodded, the light in his eyes telling her he was grasping far more than he dared to say. Her mixed race was something she'd dealt with her whole life. Her mom had been blond and blue eyed, so as soon as people saw Kiana, they knew her father was black. Her mother's backwoods Georgia family shunned her for her black blood, just like Tre and some members of her father's family had shunned her for her white blood. She'd grown up caught in the middle of two worlds, never really accepted by either.

But the man staring back at her didn't seem to curl his lip in disgust or crack a joke about her nappy hair. To him, it seemed she was more than just her race. He looked at her as though he saw beauty and nothing more.

"So did you grow up between households?" he asked,

making it sound like her parents had been divorced and sharing custody.

If only it had been as simple as that. Her father spent years denying she was his, only to rescue her when she needed him the most. "No. I lived with my mother's family until I was eight. Then Dad took me in."

"And his wife was cool with that?"

She nodded, the corners of her mouth rising up into a smile. She'd much rather talk about her relationship with her stepmother than her half-brother. "Denise has a big heart and raised me like I was her own daughter. She told me that she'd forgiven him and wouldn't hold his mistake against me."

"Sounds like a good woman."

"She is. She's as much my mom as she is Tre's."

"Is she active with the foundation?"

Kiana nodded. "As much as she can be. I think she's still grieving over Dad, and anything associated with it seems to dredge up old memories."

"I can see that." The serious Frank resurfaced for a moment. "My mom went through something similar after my dad passed away, but it gets better with time. I think keeping busy with her church and bridge club helped."

"Not to mention keeping seven boys out of trouble."

He laughed and covered her hand with his own. "Are you saying I'm trouble?"

"Most definitely." She found herself leaning closer and closer to him until their lips were inches apart.

"But only the best kind, right?"

He had no idea how correct he was. She knew the danger of giving into temptation, and yet her lips longed to touch his. Her mind cautioned that one kiss would be the beginning of a slippery slope, but her body decided it would be worth the risk. She closed her eyes and closed the gap between them.

Frank's lips were firm and demanding from the start, moving against hers with subtle variances of pressure that heated her blood and sent a thrill coursing through her veins. He kept the kiss in check, though, and that helped to rein in her own desires. They were in a public place, after all, and she needed to maintain her respectable image.

But damn, if they were behind closed doors, she definitely would've indulged in what he had to offer.

She caught the flash of a camera when she opened her eyes. The jolt chased away the warm, fuzzy feelings elicited by the kiss and left a chill of fear in its wake.

Frank laced his fingers through the hand he'd been holding and cupped her cheek with his other one. "Relax," he said in a soft, soothing voice.

"But someone just took a picture of us kissing."

"Um-hmm." He placed another of those feather-light kisses on her forehead. "Let them. Remember your plan."

Part of her wanted to pull away, but she feared what the repercussions might be if she did. "Did you just stage that kiss?"

"Nope." But the mischievous twinkle in his eyes told her he might have had something to do with the photographer.

"Frank Kelly, you are something else."

"You don't know the half of it." He placed one final kiss on the tip of her nose and pulled back. "Ready to go?"

She nodded, and he flagged the waitress for the check.

Her stomach churned, and she only wished she could've blamed it on the deep-fried goodness she'd had for lunch. Just when she'd thought she'd figured him out, some new and unexpected facet appeared. Frank Kelly was proving to be as complex and dazzling as a brilliant cut diamond. But his charm had been so blinding that she'd almost fallen for what seemed to be nothing more than an act.

He paid the check and escorted her out of the restaurant, holding the door open for her. "I think that was one of the best lunches I've had in a long time."

"Was that before or after dessert?" she asked with a healthy helping of attitude. She'd show him that she wasn't as gullible as some of the other ditzes who'd fallen for his Romeo act.

"Dessert was on a whole other level." He wrapped his arms around her, oblivious to the scene they were making on the sidewalk. "Don't you agree?"

She started to push him away, but the second her hand touched the center of his chest, she felt the rapid thudding of his heart. Despite his teasing demeanor, he was either excited or scared. "Depends."

"On what?"

"On whether we're still in the photographer's lens."

His laugh sounded a bit too tight to be casual. "Do you really care?"

She couldn't answer him right away. Part of her *did* care. She wanted to be the face of a respectable charity foundation, not some D-list celebrity trying to raise her status by sleeping with A-listers. But when he closed the space between them until their foreheads met, the urge to kiss him again almost became unbearable. The man knew how to turn the sexy on like a light switch.

"Remember that I run a charity for children," she said at last.

"Fine," he said with a playful pout before pulling back and tapping his cheek with his finger. "But can you spare just one PG-rated kiss here?"

"Gladly." She placed a peck on his cheek and waited for the next flash of a camera.

But it never came.

"Thank you." Frank took her hand and started them back toward her office building.

"So that last kiss wasn't for the camera?"

"Nope." He gave her a cheeky grin. "That was purely for me. Any time I can get a lovely lady to kiss me, I'll take it."

A player, just like her father. At least he was being honest about it. She gave him a half-hearted punch in the arm, followed by a laugh. "Something tells me I'm going to have my hands full with you."

"Oh, I'm more than a handful." A playful wag of his eyebrows added an extra layer of innuendo to his statement. "But since I'm offering my support to your foundation, I'll try to be respectable, too."

When they got back to her office, he waved to Sherita and followed Kiana into her office, closing the door behind them. For a moment, she wondered if Frank was trying to steal more than a kiss now that they were behind closed doors, but instead of taking her into his arms, he pulled out a thumb drive. "Can I give you a few files to use for your campaign?"

"What kind of files?"

"Official pics, possible quotes." He shrugged. "Stuff like that."

"But I thought you wanted to do this fake dating thing for a while before jumping on board with the foundation."

"I've seen enough already." He offered her the thumb drive again.

She took it, offering a silent prayer it didn't contain any viruses, and inserted it into the USB drive. After a quick scan for malware, she checked out the files. It contained various photos of Frank in his football uniform, just like he'd said. She clicked on one and stared at the stern countenance so at odds with the light-hearted man she'd just had lunch with. The intense glare and hard jaw belonged to a man determined to get what he wanted.

"Yeah, I know, it looks scary, but I have a rep to maintain." He took over her mouse and clicked on another photo. "I'm actually smiling in this one."

She studied it for a moment before nodding. "I'll use this one for the ads, then."

She took the mouse back, saved the file on her computer, and then dragged the image to the ad she'd been working on before he arrived.

"Jesus, what is that?" he asked.

"An ad for the gala that I need to get to the newspaper by the end of the day."

"Move over." He didn't wait for her to respond before rolling her chair out of the way and commandeering her computer. "Your spacing is all off."

He made a few changes to the layout, and her curiosity was piqued enough to let him continue.

"Will this be a color ad or black and white?" he asked,

continuing to make changes to the text.

"Color."

"Then you need to add more colors that pop, like this." He made the important text red with a golden outline, making it stand out more from the black text. "And, then, of course, you need the most important part."

He grabbed the photo of himself and placed it in the ad. A few more tweaks later, he leaned back with a satisfied smile. "Now that's more like it."

She peered over his shoulder, her lips parting in a silent gasp. The ad looked far better than she could've hoped for. "Where did you learn how to do that?"

"I was a marketing major in college." He smoothed his hands on his Notre Dame T-shirt and rose to his full height. "I may have left early to enter the draft, but I still learned a few useful things."

She glanced at the ad one more time, marveling at how he'd turned it from something blah into something she could be proud of in only a few minutes. "Thank you."

"No problem. Besides, if I'm going to put my pretty face on something, it had better look as good as me."

And just like that, the cocky player had returned.

She bit back a laugh and gave him a dramatic sigh. "Yes, you have a rep to maintain."

For a split second, his expression wavered, revealing a moment of hesitation and uncertainty. The cheeky grin took over again, but not before she'd gotten another glimpse of the man who lurked under the surface. Frank Kelly wasn't all he appeared to be, and those brief revelations eased her fear of getting mixed up with him.

"Absolutely." He took a step back and wiped his hands

45

on his shirt again, his gaze never wavering from her lips. He removed the thumb drive. "I think we have enough to get the ball rolling."

"More than enough." Especially considering the fact a picture of them kissing over dessert might already be making the rounds on the Internet.

"Then I'll check back with you next week and see if we can come up with some more ideas to promote the foundation." He straightened his shoulders, erasing the traces of vulnerability he'd displayed moments before. "Until then, lovely lady."

He left the office and said something to Sherita on the way out that set her friend off in a fit of girlish giggles. A minute later, Sherita popped into her office with a dreamy grin. "That man is all that and a bag of chips."

"Oh, he's more than just that." She nodded to the computer screen. "Take a look at what he did."

Sherita hustled over and let out a low whistle. "Brawn *and* brains."

"With a side helping of trouble." She saved the ad and sent the file to the local newspaper.

"Out with it." Her friend leaned against the desk, one balled-up hand on her hip. "I want details."

"We just had lunch."

"And I don't believe a word of that."

One of the many problems with working with a friend who'd known her since high school. Sherita could spot a lie from her like a beautician could spot a bad weave job. But how much did she dare reveal about the fake romance she was trying to cultivate? "He flirted."

"Tell me something I don't know." She fanned herself

like it was a sweltering ninety-degree day. "That man can get me hot and bothered with just a glance, but that still didn't change the fact he was only interested in you."

"He's interested in me because I'm the head of the foundation," Kiana replied, turning her attention to the emails that had arrived while she was gone.

"And I'm a virginal nun." Sherita shifted until she blocked the computer screen, her arms locked across her chest in a way that said she wasn't going to leave until she'd gotten all the juicy details.

Kiana leaned back in her desk chair with a groan. "Fine. I got him out of a bad situation in exchange for him helping me promote the gala."

"And?"

"And part of the reason he took me out to lunch was because if we're seen together in public, people will think we're dating, and it will draw more attention to the foundation and clean up his image in the process."

"Bullshit. That man has the hots for you, and he's just playing along to get past your defenses."

She sat up. "What is that supposed to mean?"

"When was the last time you went out on a date?"

She almost replied, "Just now," but instead she said, "You know why I'm not in any hurry to let a man into my life."

"No, you're just hiding behind your kid. Besides, not every man is like Malcolm. Mr. Hottie there, for example—"

"Is called 'Romeo' by his teammates for a reason," Kiana finished. "Besides, he has a temper, and I know better than to get involved with a man who knows how to

47

throw a punch."

Sherita's posture went lax, and she hung her head. "Aw, sweetie, I didn't mean it that way. I just think it's time you get back out there and remember what it's like to be a woman."

"Are you saying I'm turning into some shriveled-up prune?"

"You said it. Not me." Her friend pushed off the desk and made her way to the door. "But if I had a man like Frank Kelly chasing after me, I'd definitely indulge in a little fun while I could."

Kiana waited until she was alone before opening up the photos Frank had placed on her hard drive. The smiling version seemed to match the man who'd danced with her in the club and flirted with her over lunch. Charming. Carefree. Confident.

But when she clicked on the stern-faced version, a shiver of fear raced down her spine. This was the man who had a reputation for knocking quarterbacks to the turf on Sundays. The man who'd beaten the crap out of Malcolm and his friend and sent them both to the hospital less than a week ago.

Her pulse jumped, and a metallic taste filled her mouth, reminding her of all the times Malcolm had hit her until she tasted blood. Her hand shook as she reached for the mouse. She closed the image before it triggered a panic attack.

She'd been fooled before, but she'd learned her lesson. As much as Frank Kelly intrigued her, she needed to stay far away from him.

CHAPTER FIVE

Frank lifted the barbell with a grunt. His pulse throbbed in his temples, and his lungs burned from the effort of bench pressing two hundred and twenty-five pounds. But dammit, he was going to get to forty reps.

He only got to thirty-two before a loud bang disrupted his concentration. The force of the metal door hitting the wall behind it echoed through the nearly empty weight room, followed by the pounding of heavy footsteps. Frank had barely replaced the barbell with the trainer's assistance when Tre's angry faced loomed over him.

"What's going on with you and my sister?"

Frank's blood chilled, and a cold sweat added to the perspiration already covering his skin from his workout. The trainer wisely ducked out of the room, but there was no escape for him. He kept his voice nonchalant in the hope it would cool his friend's ire. "What are you talking about?"

"This." Tre pulled out a full-page ad from yesterday's newspaper and poked his finger right in the middle of

Frank's smiling face on it.

His anxiety waned, and he sat up slowly, wiping his face with a towel. At least Tre didn't know about the kiss. He'd asked the photographer he'd planted in the restaurant to hold off on releasing the pictures of him with Kiana. Not that it didn't keep him from pulling them up on his phone a dozen times this weekend. They looked good together. Real good. But until he got the green light from her, he was willing to respect her privacy.

"She asked me if I'd be willing to help promote your father's foundation, and I said sure."

A muscle rippled along Tre's jaw, and his hands bunched into fists, crumpling the newspaper in the process. "Fine. But keep your hands off her— understand?"

"And if she can't keep her hands off me? After all, she was the one who contacted me."

The veins along Tre's neck started to protrude, and Frank forced a laugh to break up the tension. "Relax, bro. I'll behave. Kiana's a class act, and I admire her for taking over your father's work. She's not fling material."

"Damn right, she's not." He flung the paper down and turned away, but not before Frank got the sense there was something else upsetting his teammate. The seconds ticked by, though, and Tre's fingers slowly uncurled, releasing his anger with them. "Besides, what am I worried about? I've already warned her about you, and she's smart enough to keep you at arm's length. You ain't got a chance with her. She'll push you away before letting you get too close."

"Gee, thanks." Frank took a healthy chug from the

bottle of Gatorade beside him. "Just don't ruin my chances with the rest of the ladies."

"That's all on you." Tre nodded toward the barbell. "And what are you doing here, anyway? It's the off season."

"Just trying to stay in top form." Frank stood and moved to the leg press machine. "The draft's coming up in a couple of weeks, and I want to make sure some rookie doesn't strip me of my starting position."

"Whatever, man." Tre tried to make light of the situation, but a hint of worry laced his words. If anyone was in danger of being cut, it was him.

"Want to change into some gym clothes and join me?"

Tre's phone buzzed, and his attention returned to the screen. "I've got things to do. Thinking about making a little trip to Vegas. Want to come along?"

Frank shook his head. The last time he'd joined Tre, they'd spent the whole night in the casino, either playing blackjack or watching sports scores roll in. Tre was a high roller—sometimes winning, sometimes losing—but never getting to the point where he appeared to be in over his head. "I've got too many things to do here."

"Your loss." He left the gym, his fingers flying as he replied to a text message.

Frank sat on the bench but didn't resume his workout. Something about his conversation with Tre bothered him. He meant what he'd said about Kiana not being fling material, and he knew his reputation as Romeo was a strike against him. Hell, he'd even agreed to play along with the fake romance as a way to feel out how receptive she'd be to going out with him. But if the chemistry of

51

their kiss was any indication, they'd be good together.

Real good.

However, he first needed to find out if she was interested in him or only what his name could bring to her foundation.

***

Frank stared at the number on the screen of his phone and swallowed his fear. He'd hated calling girls since junior high, and the years hadn't dulled the jumble of nerves twitching through his gut as he stood in the living room of his home and worked up the courage to press send. It would've been much easier if Kiana had been in the office when he'd swung by there this morning. Face to face, he could gauge her reaction to his invitation. Over the phone, he had no clue where he stood.

The only upside to this was that Sherita was more than willing to give him Kiana's personal cell number. If he was in the doghouse, there was no way her friend and assistant would've been so eager to share that kind of personal information. Maybe lunch last week had gone better than he thought it had.

Of course, Tre's warning from this morning still lingered in the back of his mind. Would Kiana push him away because of his reputation? Or was she only tolerating his company because of what he could do for her foundation?

There was only one way to find out. He pressed send and waited to see if she would answer.

"Hello? This is Kiana Dyer."

Damn, he loved listening to her voice. It was rich and full with just enough sass to give it a sexy vibe while still sounding professional.

He licked his lips and grasped for any shred of confidence he could get. "Hey, Kiana."

"Frank?" Her voice rose in surprise. "How did you get my number?"

"Sherita." He ran his hand along the back of his neck. Damn, this was harder than he imagined it would be. "I wanted to see how the ad was working."

The shock faded from her voice, and she seemed to slide back into that smooth, professional tone of hers. "It seems to be going well. I've been out all morning making sure we had enough tickets printed for all the people ordering them for the gala."

Some of his nerves ebbed, and he leaned back against the sofa. "So my pretty face seemed to help, huh?"

"Maybe."

He caught a hint of a teasing note and laughed, the last of his tension fading. "Glad to know I could help. Maybe there are a few more things I can do."

"Such as?"

"Well, for starters, there's that whole public persona idea."

"Are you planning on planting more photographers to catch us together?"

He grinned. If he got her to accept his invitation, he wouldn't need to hire photographers. There would be plenty on site. "Actually, I was wondering if you'd like to catch a Hawks game with me tomorrow night."

A pause filled the line, and his nerves returned with a nauseating fury. He'd rather take a hit to the gut than have her say no.

"I wish I could, but I already have plans."

His mouth went dry, and he struggled to find his voice. "No problem. My fault, actually, for asking you on such short notice."

"No, Frank, it's not that, it's just..." Her voice faded, but not before he caught an unspoken apology in it. She wanted to come, but something was keeping her from saying yes. Maybe she did have plans. Maybe she was trying to let him down gently, but at least it wasn't an outright diss.

"Some other time, then." He quickened the conversation, ready to end it as soon as possible. "I'll check back with you later this week to brainstorm some more ideas for fundraising."

"I—" She caught herself and then changed her response. "Thank you."

The call ended, and he stared at his phone, wishing he knew why she'd said no.

***

Kiana's heart fluttered like a hummingbird on crack as she ended Frank's call. For a split second, she'd been tempted to say yes. But then she'd spied her daughter's picture on her desk and remembered why she couldn't indulge in the sinful temptation that was Frank Kelly.

"So what did Frank want?" Sherita asked from the doorway.

"Why don't you start by telling me how he got my phone number?" She'd barely walked back into her office when the phone rang, and now that the call was over, she finished unloading her briefcase.

Her friend looked up at the ceiling and buffed her

shiny ruby-colored nails on her blouse. "Well, he said it was urgent."

"I should've known you were behind this."

"And I want to know what you turned down." Sherita crossed the room and sat on the edge of Kiana's desk. "And maybe afterward, we can get your head examined for telling him no."

Kiana closed her eyes and counted to ten. She'd hoped her best friend would understand why she refused to get tangled up with someone like Frank, not try to play matchmaker. "I might need to change my number."

"Stop changing the subject. It's not like he was asking you over to his place for a night of wild, hot, sweaty sex." A mischievous glint filled her dark eyes, and she leaned forward. "Or did he?"

"He asked me to go to a Hawks game with him tomorrow night."

"And you turned him down?" Sherita's brows furrowed. "Girl, what's wrong with you? You love basketball."

"Yes, but who's going to take care of Savannah?"

"Is that why you said no?" She shook her head and crossed her arms. "What about that nanny of yours?"

Kiana knew she was just making excuses, but it was better than risking another night in Frank's presence. The fake relationship was turning out to be a dangerous idea. If he ended the evening with an invitation to go back to his place, she doubted she'd have the strength to say no. "Madison needs time off, too. I can't ask her to stay late on such short notice."

"Then *I'll* watch your baby girl."

"Sherita, please, I can't ask that of you."

"Why? Don't you trust me?"

"I do, but…" She released a heavy sigh and let her empty bag fall to the floor. Time to call uncle. Her friend wasn't going to let up until she told her the real reason why she'd turned Frank down. "The truth is, I'm not ready to risk getting involved with anyone right now."

"Who says you'd be getting involved? He just asked you to a basketball game, not a weekend on some 'clothing is optional' private island."

"But you said it yourself—that man can get you hot and bothered with just a glance, and I've been so removed from the playing field, I don't know what he wants. Maybe he just wants to hang out. Maybe he wants more. I have no idea."

"There's only one way to find out." Sherita held out Kiana's cell phone. "There's a nice little feature that lets you call back the last person who called you."

Kiana held the phone for a moment and stared at it before looking back to her friend. "Are you sure you can handle Savannah for a few hours?"

"That baby of yours is an angel."

"I promise to come home right after the game."

"And miss out on a little one-on-one action with Frank Kelly?" Sherita cocked one brow up in challenge. "You disappoint me."

"I'm taking things nice and slow."

"Fine, so long as you take him up on his offer. Now call him before he finds someone else to take to that game."

Kiana waited until Sherita returned to her desk before

hitting the redial button.

It rang several times before a smooth, suave voice answered, "Changed your mind?"

Damn that man and his cockiness. It did little to quiet the jolt of anticipation jumping around in the pit of her stomach when she imagined him using the same tone in the bedroom. "Actually, I was able to move some things around and free up tomorrow night." She licked her lips and offered a silent prayer she really didn't sound as desperate as she felt. "That is, if the invitation is still open."

"Of course." She could almost hear him grinning on the other end of the line. "Should I pick you up at your place?"

"No." Panic tightened her throat. It was one thing for him to know where she worked, but her home was strictly off limits. "The office is closer."

"And what about dinner beforehand?"

If lunch last Friday was any indication, dinner might result in them skipping the game entirely for a completely different type of sporting event. The minute his lips touched hers, all common sense flew out the window. "Sorry, but I'll be working up until tip-off."

She didn't miss the disappointment in his voice as he asked, "What time should I pick you up?"

"Game starts at seven thirty, so with traffic, six forty-five should be fine."

"Sounds like a plan." The easy confidence flowed back into his words. "I look forward to tomorrow night."

"So do I." Her reply slipped through before she could catch herself, and embarrassment burned her cheeks. So much for keeping her attraction to him in check.

He chuckled, and the sound soothed her rattled nerves. "That makes two of us. See you at six forty-five."

He hung up, and she reached for her bottle of water. Forget getting hot and bothered from a glance. The man managed to turn her on with just his voice.

As she chugged her water, she didn't miss Sherita giggling from the other room. "Girl, you're in over your head," her friend called out.

"And it's all your fault," she shot back.

But if she was going to get mixed up with the likes of Frank Kelly, at least she'd have a good time doing it.

CHAPTER SIX

Frank let out a low whistle when he entered Kiana's office. He'd been expecting her to still be in her prim and proper office attire, but the skin-tight jeans molded that perfect ass of hers in ways that made him forget his own name.

"Good evening," she said with a shy smile.

"Oh, baby, it's getting better all the time." He placed a chaste kiss on her cheek and took a moment to drag his gaze away from that pert bottom and soak in the rest of her appearance. A form-fitting jersey was layered over a long-sleeved red T-shirt and outlined the generous curves underneath. Her soft curls framed her face, and a pair of blue stiletto heels with the team's logo on them completed the outfit. It was the perfect balance of sporty and sexy, and for a moment, he considered taking her back to his place for some bedroom athletics instead of the game.

Cool your jets, he warned himself. *This is Kiana, not some bimbo you hit up at a party.*

He resisted the urge to tug at the collar of his shirt and

forced a confident smile on his face. "You look awesome."

"Sorry if I went a little overboard, but I'm a huge fan." She ran her hands over her hair. "I just hope my hair isn't so big that it blocks the view of the people sitting behind us."

"It's fine." He twirled one curl around his finger, marveling at how soft and silky it was. Most of the black women in Atlanta paid outrageous sums to straighten their hair, but not Kiana. It served to soften her normally sharp and polished appearance. "It fits you."

"What is that supposed to mean?"

"It means you're beautiful without trying too hard."

She laughed. "You have no idea how much work goes into looking this way."

"Well, it's definitely appreciated." He offered his arm. "Let's go before the game starts without us."

As they waited for the elevator, he remembered a conversation he'd had with his father when he was a teenager. His father had said there were girls you took to bed, and there were girls you took home to meet your mother. Ideally, he'd look for one who fit into both categories when he decided to settle down.

Kiana definitely fit that description. From the moment he saw her, he wanted to get her naked, but as he spent more time with her, his respect for her grew. She was definitely one he wanted to treat like a lady because if she only felt a fraction of the attraction he did, he didn't want to ruin his chances with her.

He led her down to the parking garage and held the passenger door of his Maserati Quattroporte. "Ladies first."

She slid into the leather seat and admired the interior. "Nice ride."

"It's not as flashy as the Lamborghinis some of the other guys have, but it's still fast." He closed the door and jogged around the car. This was as nerve-wracking as a real first date. "Ready for some fun?"

She gave him a grin that said, "game on."

He revved up the engine and tore out of the parking garage as fast as he dared.

A squeal broke free from Kiana's lips, but the flush in her cheeks told him it was more from delight than fear. The interstate was still a mess of rush-hour traffic, so he was forced to stick to the side streets as he made his way down from Midtown to Phillips Arena. Not the best way to show off what his car could do, but maybe after the game...

He glanced at Kiana and wondered if she'd be open to a little late-night fun with him.

The blare of a car horn jerked his attention back to the road. Thankfully, he wasn't the driver at fault, but the incident rattled him enough to stay focused on one thing at a time.

That didn't keep him from making small talk with her. "Have you been to many games this season?"

She shook her head. "Been too busy. I used to go all the time with Dad, though."

A pang of sadness lingered in her voice, and he silently cursed. The last thing he wanted to do was dredge up some unpleasant memories. "Are you sure you want to go? Because if—"

"Of course I want to go." She looked at him with confusion. "I wouldn't have accepted your invitation if I didn't."

"I know how some places have special meanings to people, and I didn't want to take you anywhere that would make you miss him." He rubbed the back of his neck and hoped she wouldn't ask any more about it.

Of course, she was too smart not to pick up on what he said. "You sound like you're speaking from experience."

He shrugged and waited for her to change the subject.

"What's your story, Frank Kelly?"

He gripped the steering wheel and weighed the pros and cons of revealing the truth to her. He had a reputation as a tough guy, as an aggressive linebacker who knocked opponents to the turf on a regular basis. "Just that I get that certain places have sentimental value."

"What's your place?"

"Soldier Field." He gave her a sheepish smile. "There's a reason I won't play for the Bears. Every time I set foot in that stadium, I remember all the games I went there with my dad. We played a game there once while I was at Notre Dame, and when I went out on the field, I just froze. I couldn't get my head on straight until halfway through the second quarter."

"You missed him that much?"

"I'm sure it had something to do with the fact it was only a few months after he'd died." His throat choked up. "But yeah, I miss him. I gave him way too much grief when he was alive."

"I think we all give our parents grief at one time or

another."

"No, I was by far the biggest troublemaker out of all my brothers. I blame the red hair," he added, cracking a joke and pointing to the one feature that made him stand out among his siblings.

"Yeah, redheads do have a reputation for hot tempers." She sounded like she was trying to be flippant, but he didn't miss the way she squirmed in her seat.

Shit! After witnessing the way her ex so casually backhanded her at the club, he began to wonder if there was more to their history. If that asshole had hit her before...

He squeezed the steering wheel until his knuckles turned white. Then he caught himself. He could only imagine what he looked like to her right now. Probably something close to the Hulk in a smashing rage.

Frank forced himself to think of more pleasant things, and his anger faded. "So, is this a fake date or an official date?"

"Excuse me?" The sassy attitude returned with the same force as the moment he'd met her at the club.

"You know. You and me, being seen in public together, trying to raise awareness for the foundation. Is it going to be all business? Or will you allow yourself a few moments of pleasure?"

She responded with a squinty-eyed glare.

He laughed it off. "Hey, you can't blame me for trying. I'd have to be gay not to be attracted to a woman like you."

"Oh, really?"

"Absolutely." He gave her a quick once-over, admiring

every inch of her. "You're smart, kind, generous, and so friggin' sexy that I have to remind myself every few minutes to be a gentleman in your presence."

"Who says I want a gentleman?" she teased.

All the blood rushed to his dick. Now it was his turn to squirm uncomfortably in his seat. "So you're giving me permission to turn this into a real date?"

"We'll see, Romeo."

He grinned. A challenge had just been laid down. One he gladly accepted. She'd left the door open just wide enough to allow him to charm her off her feet. Now to put his plan into action.

***

Kiana stopped short when Frank pointed to the leather-covered, courtside chairs between the benches. "Holy shit, Frank. Those are the Hollywood seats."

"I know," he replied with the nonchalant ease of someone who routinely got the best of everything.

"But how did you get them?"

"You're not the only person who knows people in high places." He gave her a wink and took her hand. "Now let's sit down and enjoy the game."

Her head swam from the extravagance of it, but Frank had no problem flagging a member of the dance team and asking for a Coke. The request jerked her from her stunned silence. "She's a cheerleader, not a waitress."

"One of the perks of these seats is that you get a member of the dance team to bring you whatever you want." He shrugged. "I figured a soda was safer than a beer. Do you want anything?"

When the dancer returned, she gave Frank a smile that

64

said she would be more than happy to bring him whatever he wanted.

A wave of jealousy rose within Kiana, and she looped her arm through his and glared at the girl.

Frank chuckled. "Making a claim on me?"

"More like telling her not to offer you a lap dance while you're the celebrity face of my foundation." True, their relationship—if she dared to call it that—was nothing more than a farce designed to drum up publicity for her fundraising gala. But she couldn't ignore the trickle of heat that made its way down her spine and settled in the pit of her stomach.

As the game got under way, though, the unease vanished. Kiana became swept up in the action long enough to forget that this was a fake date. The conversation flowed so easily between her and Frank, it was as though they were old friends. For a football player, he knew as much about basketball as she did—maybe more.

Near the end of the second quarter, a member of the opposing team elbowed a player going up for a rebound, and the ref failed to call the foul. Kiana jumped to her feet and shouted, "How could you have missed that?"

A strong hand took hers and pulled her back into her seat. "They don't need you on the court."

"But that ref is blind." She shook free of him, her body twitching with pent-up rage. "How the hell could he let that slide?"

Frank's blue eyes twinkled, and he grinned. "Who's the hothead now?"

"But you saw that, right?"

"Yeah, but refs make bad calls all the time. Arguing with them only makes things worse. Trust me—I know."

She crossed her arms and slumped back in her seat. There was no way she was going to win this argument with him staying as cool as a cucumber.

The second quarter ended, and just before the team went to the lockers for halftime, one of the players nodded to Frank. "'Sup, Kelly?"

"Just watching you guys play like girls, Dougie," he teased.

Kiana's jaw dropped for the second time that evening. It was one thing to have a conversation with a member of your favorite team, but to crack a joke at his expense?

Doug laughed it off and went into the locker room.

Once he left, Kiana gave Frank a light smack in the center of his chest. "You know Doug Boutry?"

"Yeah, why?" Frank replied, his brows drawing together in puzzlement.

"Because he's one of the stars of the team."

Frank's face relaxed into an easy smile. "Maybe, but he sucks at playing *Halo*."

"Hold on a minute." Her mind still whirled from everything she'd witnessed so far tonight. Her dad had been a legend, but it still didn't seem to get him into the same circles Frank moved in. "You play video games with him?"

Frank nodded. "So?"

She opened her mouth to speak, but no words came out. Once again, Frank Kelly had managed to render her speechless.

"Want to meet him after the game?" he offered.

Her tongue continued to be a clumsy blob in her mouth. "Seriously?"

"Yeah, if you want." He leaned closer and lowered his voice to a whisper. "I'll talk him into playing a game of one-on-one with you if it will score me some brownie points."

She didn't know whether or not to believe him, so she chose to roll her eyes instead. "Sure, Frank."

"No, I'll prove it." He started to rise, but it was her turn to yank him back into his seat.

Her heart hammered so hard from just the idea of meeting one of her favorite players that she was certain she'd keel over from a heart attack if she actually did. "Maybe later. I need to get home and get some sleep before going into work tomorrow."

"Just let me know what works for you, and I'll arrange it. Anything for you, lovely lady," he added with a wink and smile.

The return of the flirtatious Frank soothed her rattled nerves and brought them back to the relaxed vibe they'd enjoyed earlier, and her lips rose into a matching grin. "You just don't give up, do you?"

He shook his head and waited for the dance team to finish their routine before ordering another round of Cokes from the girl designated to serve them that evening.

At the end of the third quarter, the dreaded Kiss Cam made an appearance on the screen. Frank nudged her and said, "You know, my brother met his future wife because of one of those."

"Are you telling the truth, or is this a load of blarney?"

His eyes widened in mock innocence, and he crossed

his heart. "It's the truth."

She was about to roll her eyes again, but someone behind them tapped her shoulder. She followed his finger to the big screen and stared at her image.

Frank leaned in and murmured in her ear, "Shall we give them a good show?"

She licked her lips. After all, it was just a show. A publicity stunt she'd come up with to help get some attention for her father's foundation. What damage would one little kiss do?

Kiana closed the space between them, aiming for a demure peck on the cheek, but Frank intercepted her by locking his lips on hers.

Sweet Jesus! It was ten times more intense than the kiss they'd shared over lunch. Fire, passion, heat—it was all there for her delight. She closed her eyes and indulged in what he offered her, savoring the warmth of his touch and the sugary sweetness of the Coke that lingered on his lips. It infected her to the point where she gathered his shirt in her hand and fought the urge to rip it off.

And yet, despite the intensity of it all, Frank still managed to keep it PG rated. His tongue never got involved, much to her dismay, and after they'd gotten a chorus of cheers from the audience, he managed to pull away. "Careful, Kiana," he said in a tight voice. "Remember the kids."

She opened her eyes and blinked several times to clear the lust-filled haze that clouded her vision. When things came into focus, she found Frank staring at her with something akin to a grimace.

"What's wrong?"

"Nothing." His chest rose and fell at the same breathless rate as hers. "Just fighting the urge not to sling you over my shoulder and take you somewhere more private so we can really kiss."

"Are you saying you didn't stage that kiss like the other one?"

"Nope." He turned and faced the court. "And if you had been anyone else, they'd have to censor that kiss."

"Meaning?"

He turned back to her and arched one brow. "Do I need to show you how turned on I am by you? It's turning into pure torture trying to behave when I'm around you."

"And why are you trying so hard to behave?"

"Because until you decide you want to make things real, I'm minding my manners."

His answer caught her off guard. Maybe this wasn't all a show to Frank. Lord knows, he didn't kiss like a man out to fake a relationship. Too bad she wasn't in a place where she could make things real between them. If things had been different, she'd have no problem letting her guard down and going out with him. But she was no longer the carefree woman she'd once been. She had responsibilities, obligations, a reputation to uphold. And none of those allowed her to get involved with Frank Kelly.

Silence replaced the easy conversations they'd enjoyed earlier, and as Frank walked her back to his car after the game, he stared at the ground and shuffled his feet along the concrete. "Did I overstep my bounds, Kiana?"

"No," she replied with a bit of caution.

She waited for him to open the car door, but he braced his outstretched arm against the window beside her.

"Then let me just clear the air for a minute. I like you, Kiana. A lot. Too much, actually. And I'd like to go out with you, even after this whole fundraiser thing is over. But if you don't feel the same way, then please let me know now so I don't say or do anything that will earn me a slap in the face."

Her mind listed a dozen reasons why she shouldn't engage him, but her body had different ideas. She arched against him, her body against the hard contours of his muscles, and captured his cheeks between her hands. "How about you give me one of those kisses that need to be censored?"

"As you wish."

She'd expected something playful or flirtatious from him, but from the second his mouth engaged hers, she was left breathless. This wasn't a kiss for pure show. It was real. No reservations. No acting. No holding back. Just pure, raw desire playing out with every movement of his lips.

He silently pleaded for her to open her mouth, and when she did, a moan of pleasure escaped from her. Damn, the boy could kiss. His arm circled her waist and held her against him while his tongue performed a forbidden dance that made her crave a night filled with naked bodies and tangled sheets. She breathed him in, the scent of his aftershave heightening her desire until she forgot about everything but him.

Then he cupped his hand along the back of her neck, and a painful rush of memories overtook any pleasure she might have known. A chill rippled through her veins. She jerked back with a gasp, reminded of all the times Malcolm had grabbed her there and squeezed the muscles at the base her skull just before he struck her.

"Kiana?" Frank asked, his voice filled with worry.

It was enough to pull her from the flashbacks, but not enough to tame the trembling in her hands. She hid them behind her back and leaned against the car, fighting the tears that gathered in the corners of her eyes. Her breaths shook with choked-back sobs. "I'm sorry."

"For what?"

She didn't want to tell him about that chapter of her life, of the months she'd cowered and let a man physically and emotionally beat her. She'd been strong enough to get away from Malcolm, but it was still very clear that she hadn't been able to put the past behind her. Her voice shook as she replied, "Please, Frank, just take me back to the office."

Concern filled his blue eyes, followed by confusion and then resignation. "Of course."

He opened the door, and she sank into her seat. Shame replaced her terror, and she couldn't bring herself to meet his gaze as they drove back into the city.

Several minutes ticked by before Frank asked, "He hit you, didn't he? The asshole in the club?"

She turned to him, ready to ask how he knew, but the murderous expression on his face silenced her.

"I only wish I beat him harder than I did." Frank's hands gripped the steering wheel in white-knuckled rage. "Men like him don't deserve any mercy."

"Frank—" Her voice caught, and she turned back to the window. "It's in the past."

"Maybe, but it obviously still bothers you."

"It's my problem, not yours."

"Bullshit." He punched the accelerator of his Maserati, and it took off with enough force to push her back against her seat. His anger waned as the speedometer rose, and he added, "You know I would never do that to you, right?"

Did she? The man who made a living out of tackling grown men to the ground? The man who'd broken her ex's jaw with a series of well-placed punches?

And yet, for all his history of violence, he'd been nothing but calm and considerate to her. If she ignored the scene at the club and what she'd seen on the TV every Sunday during football season, she'd almost believe he didn't have a mean bone in his body.

When she didn't answer right away, a whispered curse flew from his lips, and his shoulders slumped in defeat. "Never mind."

"Like I said, it's not you. It's me." She shivered in spite of the warm evening. "Some things are just harder to forget than others, and when you touched me there…"

Now it was her turn to mutter a curse under her breath. She hated revealing her vulnerability to him. She wanted to present the self-assured, confident, indestructible side of herself to Frank, not the weak, flawed version she'd become when she'd dated Malcolm. "Please, let's just change the subject, okay?"

"Fine." The terse manner in which he said the word, though, showed he was anything but fine with ending the conversation that way, along with the way his car wove in and out of traffic as though the Downtown Connector was a NASCAR speedway. "Let's talk about the fundraiser. I saw there was going to be a silent auction of some sports memorabilia."

Finally, something she could talk to him about that didn't make her horny or scared. "We have a few things of my dad's."

"I'll gladly donate a couple of things, too, but I was wondering if you're willing to open it up to sports other than football."

"What do you mean?"

The car slowed back down to the flow of traffic, and his grip loosened on the steering wheel. "Well, football's not the only sport where kids can get hurt."

"We focus primarily on football, but we can supply gear to all youth sports programs."

"Exactly, so why don't I ask around and see if I can get some other local athletes involved in the fundraiser. Dougie, for example."

Her heart stuttered for a few beats. "You mean you could get Doug Boutry to donate something to the auction?"

"Of course I can." He gave her a charming grin. "You'll find I can be pretty convincing. And it wouldn't be limited to just Doug. I can ask my teammates to provide a few things, maybe even get the team's owners to provide a couple of seats in the suite for a game. Just tell me what I need to do, and I'll do it."

She wiped her damp palms on her jeans as she considered his offer. "You'd be willing to do that for me?"

"Anything to stay on your good side." He took the Midtown exit near her office. "I'm just surprised you didn't think of it before."

A dozen excuses sat poised on the tip of her tongue,

but it was the most honest one that came out. "I have a hard time asking people for help."

"And yet, you asked me," he said softly.

"Yeah, but I had some leverage over you."

"I would've done it even if you hadn't bailed me out."

She chuckled, and the last of the cold dread fled her soul, leaving behind an odd sensation she couldn't quite pinpoint. There was a sincerity to Frank's words that made her wonder how much of it was the truth. "For the record, I never bailed you out."

"You got me out of the slammer, and that's what counts." His grin widened. "Can you imagine what someone as good looking as me would've had to endure if I'd stayed in there?"

His good-natured conceit lightened the mood, and she laughed wholeheartedly. Leave it to Frank to take her from one end of the emotional spectrum to the other in a matter of minutes. But it felt good, being with him. Even after she'd revealed her shortcomings, he'd managed to make her feel better. And he showed no evidence of losing interest in her, judging by the way his gaze kept flickering her way as he zoomed through the streets.

He drove into the parking garage of her building and parked next to her car. Before she could even grab the handle of her door, he was out of his seat and jogging around the car to open it for her. "Allow me, lovely lady."

"Still trying to get on my good side?" she quipped while smothering a grin.

"You can say that." He took her hand to help her out, but didn't release it right away. His eyes darkened, and his face grew uncharacteristically serious. "Kiana, if I'm going too far, please tell me."

Her breath hitched, allowing his scent to linger in her nose long enough for her to recognize the masculine notes of leather and cedar in his cologne. "Depends on what you're planning to do."

"Can we try that kiss again?" He held up his hands in surrender. "I promise not to lay a finger on you."

That kiss had been nice. At least, until he touched the back of her neck. But maybe, just maybe, she could enjoy one more. She leaned into him and pressed her lips to his.

If the earlier kiss had been raw and unrestrained, this one was gentle and cautious. And frustratingly tame. Frank allowed her to control the tempo and the heat of the kiss, responding to the demands of her tongue, but obviously holding back. She opened one eye to see his hands shaking at his sides. A whimper rose from his throat, forming a silent plea that convinced her to tear down the wall he was trying to stay behind.

She grabbed his hands and placed them on her bottom.

A muffled gasp followed, and the chains that had been holding Frank at bay vanished. He grabbed her ass with vigor and pressed her against him while he deepened the kiss. A moan rose into the still night air, but she couldn't tell if it was from him or her. All she knew was the rising desire building between them that made her want to forget everything but him.

She allowed herself this one moment of bliss, to fall into the arms of a man who knew how to kiss her in a way that made her toes curl. A man who caressed her generous curves like she was the most desirable woman on earth. A man who made her feel safe and secure in his arms even while he tempted her to engage in the most reckless behavior she'd embraced in over two years.

But she couldn't be reckless anymore. She was a mother, and she didn't want to make the same mistakes her mother had. The thought of her daughter tempered her lust long enough for her to end the kiss before it got out of hand.

"Damn, Kiana," Frank said with shuddering breaths. "You have the most luscious ass I've ever held."

He gave her behind one more squeeze as though to prove his point, and she laughed. Frank Kelly would never be the serious sort of guy she needed to settle down with, but he was definitely amusing enough to keep around. She gave him one final peck on the lips before prying his hands off her skin-tight jeans. "I have a meeting at eight in the morning."

"And I have a few favors to call in." He moved to her car. "Give me a few days to pull everything together."

Finding her keys, she opened her door and started the engine. "I'm grateful for anything you can do to help the foundation."

"I'm not just doing it for the foundation." His eyes never left her face as he closed her door and stepped back. Even in silence, he drove his point home. He wanted her.

Her pulse quickened, and she drove away before she lost all common sense and invited him back to her place for what would most certainly be a night of orgasmic sex. But would the pleasure be worth the pain that would follow?

No, it was better to be safe. He was trying to stay on her good side, and she needed to stay on his, especially if he followed through on his offer. Launching headfirst into a purely physical relationship with him would leave her breathless, but in the end, they'd have to go their separate ways. Romeo would add another notch on his headboard while she'd go back to being the responsible adult she had to be for both Savannah and the foundation.

It just wasn't worth the risk.

But that still didn't keep her from lying awake in her cold, lonely bed and replaying how good it had felt to be in his arms.

CHAPTER SEVEN

Kiana watched Savannah on the nanny cam as her daughter teetered across the floor and climbed onto her unicorn rocking horse. Madison, her nanny, cheered as the twenty-month-old moved back and forth without assistance.

At her desk, Kiana clapped and cheered, wishing she could be there to witness it in person instead of on a computer screen. Her daughter never ceased to amaze her. Every day brought something new. And she hoped Savannah would one day grow up to be a confident young woman who knew the value of her own self-worth.

But in order to teach her that, I need to demonstrate it for her.

Which meant back to work. If she could turn this foundation into a success, she'd be one step closer to becoming the role model she wanted to be for her daughter.

She clicked off the nanny cam and opened a spreadsheet. The first page contained the costs of the gala, all in the red. But the second sheet made her smile. It showed that the number of tickets sold had more than tripled since they'd placed the ad with Frank's picture last Sunday. Not bad for two weeks' worth of work, especially considering the large spike that had occurred since she'd gone to the game with him ten days ago.

Of course, she hadn't heard a peep from him since then, either. He'd said he needed a few days to round up some items for the auction, but his silence raised all kinds of doubts. Like, had she scared him away by mentioning her history with Malcolm? Or had her reaction to him touching the back of her neck made him question getting involved with a basket case like her?

She lowered her head to her desk and heaved a heavy sigh. As much as she wanted to keep things professional, he'd managed to get under her skin. That last kiss just sealed the deal. And ten lonely nights had done nothing to ease the ache of desire that flared every time she replayed it.

Focus, girl. You have more important things to worry about than him.

She lifted her head and smoothed her hair back just a split second before she heard the low rumble of a man's voice outside her office. She glanced at her screen to make sure the nanny cam window was closed.

Sherita's high-pitched laughter filled the office when Frank opened the door. He wore his usual flirtatious grin and laughed back. "Just think about it," he said before turning his attention to Kiana. "Good morning, lovely lady."

"Do you ever lay off the charm?" she asked, rising from her chair.

"Nope. It's encoded in my DNA." He winked and held out a file folder. "I just wanted to stop by and show you my progress."

She took the folder and opened it. The first page was a spreadsheet listing the items donated by Frank's team members. The second page listed items from the Hawks, including a signed jersey from Doug Boutry. The rest of the pages were pictures of the items.

Her throat choked up as she went through them. "Frank, this is amazing!"

"It's just the start." He sat down at the desk and took over her mouse. "I've talked with a local tech company here, and they've set up an online auction site for you to use since we'll probably run out of space in the ballroom at the rate we're going."

A few clicks later, she was staring at a professional website listing some of the items in the folder. "Frank, it's too much."

"No, it's not." His expression grew serious. "When I sign up to do something, I never give less than a hundred and ten percent. And I'm just getting warmed up."

"But why?"

"I thought the answer was obvious." His voice softened, and his gaze fell to her lips.

Before she knew what was happening, she had moved between him and the desk. What started out as a simple kiss of appreciation quickly morphed into the same wild and unrestrained passion from the other night. She threaded her fingers through his short hair and teased the opening of his mouth with her tongue. She wasted no time once he granted her access to it, tasting the hint of peppermint toothpaste that lingered inside. She breathed in his clean scent and fell further into the blissful insanity of desire.

Frank stood and cupped her ass in his hands before lifting her up on the desk. Then he pushed her dress up until it was bunched around her hips. With gentle hands, he guided her legs around his waist while he ground against her, each movement of his hips replicating what she wanted him to do to her in the bedroom. He paused long enough to murmur her name in a sexy growl that only made her want him even more before kissing her senseless once again.

She locked her ankles around him and pressed him as tightly against her as she could. With their previous kisses, she'd held back, ever fearful someone would catch her losing control like this. But behind the closed door of her office, she didn't fear getting caught by anyone other than Sherita, and she already knew her best friend would only cheer her on if she walked in on them.

Frank squeezed her ass. "Damn it, Kiana. I don't know how much longer I can keep being a gentleman when you kiss me like that."

"Then what would you do?" she asked.

His pupils expanded, and the heat in his voice sent delicious shivers down her spine. "You know exactly what I'd do. I'd strip you naked. Then I'd taste every inch of your skin." He paused to draw her earlobe into his mouth and flick his tongue over it, earning another shiver from her. "Then, once I had you hot and wet and ready for me, I'd make you come so hard, you'd be left sated and exhausted until morning."

"And then what?"

His low chuckle made her insides quiver in anticipation. "And then I'd do it all over again."

Now she understood why his teammates called him Romeo, because she was more than ready to surrender to him and let him carry out his promises right there on her desk.

Thankfully, the pause allowed her to hear another voice.

Her brother's.

A chill of fear washed over her, and she pushed Frank away. A glance at the clock said it was eleven thirty. "Shit! I forgot that Tre and Denise were coming over for lunch."

She jumped off the desk and pulled her dress down. Her cheeks burned, and a quick glance in the mirror revealed a guilty flush and undeniably swollen lips. All they'd have to do was take one look at her to know exactly what she and Frank had been doing moments before. And she wasn't ready to announce that she and Frank were an item, especially when she wasn't sure where their so-called relationship stood.

At least Sherita seemed to be stalling them, judging by the conversation on the other side of the door.

For his part, Frank didn't seem too mussed up from their makeout session. His shirt had managed to stay neatly tucked in, and his closely cropped hair showed no signs of the disorder her fingers had caused when she'd run them through it moments before. He stepped back with a wince and covered the bulge in his jeans with the file folder, his chest still rising and falling faster than normal.

But thankfully, by the time Tre and Denise entered her office, she and Frank had managed to get themselves in order.

Her brother stopped short when he saw his teammate, his eyes narrowing. "What are you doing here?"

"Just showing Kiana something I've been working on." He squared his shoulders and stared at Tre like he had every right to be there. "I was demonstrating a few things I'd like to try. That is, if she was open to the idea."

A new wave of heat rose into her cheeks, and she stared at the top of her desk. If he followed through on what he promised, she was more than open to the idea. Unfortunately, a night of pleasure in his bed had nothing to do with the foundation she needed to run during the day.

The staring match intensified, only now she was bearing some of the anger from Tre's glare. Time to diffuse it before the boys got into a fistfight.

After she introduced Frank to Denise, she beckoned her brother and stepmother over to her computer. "Come see what Frank set up for the foundation."

Denise came over first and smiled when she saw the auction website. She clicked through some of the listings, her smile widening. "Look at all the items!"

That was all Tre needed to end his silent standoff. He joined his mother at the computer screen. "Where did you get all this?"

"I just asked around," Frank replied with a shrug. "I have a few more things in works, though."

His gaze fell on Kiana in an unspoken dare that asked if she was up to accepting his offer.

She turned away before he saw how tempted she was. Her heart hammered in her chest, but she managed to keep her voice level as she said, "The online auction might be a good idea. It will raise awareness for the foundation beyond the local level and help us raise more funds."

"I couldn't agree more." Denise placed her hand on Frank's arm and smiled up at him. "We can't thank you enough for all you've done."

Frank turned his charming grin on her. "I'm just getting started, Mrs. Dyer. Your husband was an inspiration to me, and this is my chance to pay it forward."

"And what else are you planning on doing?" Tre asked in a way that clearly said *keep your hands off my sister.*

"Depends on when Kiana tells me to stop."

Her pulse went into overdrive. Oh, dear Lord, would these boys just grow up? "So far, I'm liking everything Frank's done."

And that includes what was happening a few minutes ago.

Frank caught the underlying meaning of her answer and bounced on his heels. "Good to know, because as I mentioned, I have a few more things up my sleeve."

"Such as?" Tre asked, his frown deepening.

"My brother is asking some of his hockey buddies for items, for example. After all, hockey gear can be pricey, but the kids still need good brain buckets if they want to play."

The boy was so good at playing the innocent act, Kiana wondered how many times he'd gotten away with it. At least it kept her from getting a tongue lashing from her brother, although she'd probably hear about it later once Frank left.

Denise, however, remained the peacekeeper. "And the foundation would gladly fund any youth hockey programs in need."

"I'll pass that on to Ben so he can drum up some more support."

Tre's expression darkened into something akin to jealousy. "Well, that's nice and all, but we have lunch reservations."

It was his way of ending the conversation before Frank got any more praise, but Kiana was grateful they had a reason to leave. Any more time in Frank's presence, and she might forget herself.

"Would you like to join us?" Denise asked.

Frank took one look at Tre before shaking his head. "Thank you, Mrs. Dyer, but I have a plane to catch."

That got her attention. Kiana lifted her gaze to him, trying to decipher what the next step in his plan was. "Where are you going?"

"Orlando," he replied as though he were just taking a jaunt to another part of the city. "The Braves are down there for spring training, after all."

Her jaw dropped, which was the only reason why she didn't say anything when he kissed her cheek and made his way to the door.

"I'll be in touch," Frank said with a wave before leaving the office.

"Such a nice young man," Denise said.

"He's anything but that." Tre's hands tightened into fists. "What exactly are you up to?"

"What do you mean?" If Frank could play innocent, so could she.

"You know exactly what I mean." He grabbed her keyboard and entered in a web address.

A picture of her and Frank kissing at the Hawks game appeared on the screen.

Kiana's foot twitched, and her tongue tumbled over an appropriate answer. "It was for the Kiss Cam."

"Uh-huh." The tone in his voice said he didn't believe her. "I've already warned you once, but I'm going to warn you again. Stay away from Frank. He's nothing but a player."

Kiana closed her eyes and took a deep breath. "I know, I know."

"Then why are you falling for his line of bullshit?"

"Watch your language," Denise snapped. "And last I checked, Kiana was a grown woman who is capable of making her own choices."

"Yeah, and look at her track record. She's just like her white trash mama."

"Don't talk to your sister that way. I raised you better than that." Denise glared at Tre, who responded by lowering his eyes.

But the damage had been done. Tre's accusation hit her like a blow to the chest. The line of men that streamed through her mother's bedroom. The loud arguments that sometimes ended with slaps and punches and broken furniture. And then the night where the sound of a single gunshot ended it all. "Please, Tre, you don't have to remind me."

"Good, because I want to bring up one more thing. You've got to think of that little girl of yours. How do you think Frank's going to react when you tell him about

Savannah?"

She bit her bottom lip and looked away.

"I thought so." Tre crossed his arms over his puffed-out chest. "You know as well as I do he's not someone you want around her, so you'd better keep that in mind the next time Romeo tests out his moves on you."

She wilted inside. Tre was right. Frank might be one hell of a kisser, but he'd probably take off running the moment he learned she had a kid. That is, if she ever trusted him enough to tell him about Savannah. She'd gone to great lengths to protect her daughter from her ex, and that included limiting the number of people who knew where she was or even of her existence. She refused to drag Savannah into the hell that had been her own childhood with the revolving door of her mother's "boyfriends." She had to be better than her mother.

"Point made," she muttered.

"Good. Now let's go before they give away our table." Tre led the way out of the office, but Denise trailed alongside her.

A sympathetic smile lingered on the older woman's lips. "Don't listen to him, Kiana. Listen to your heart and your gut. Between the two of them, they'll never steer you wrong."

The problem was, her heart and her gut were at odds. Her gut warned her to keep Frank Kelly at arm's length, but her heart wondered if there was more to him than the player he pretended to be.

CHAPTER EIGHT

Frank breathed in the balmy central Florida air that was scented with orange blossoms. The sun had set hours ago, but the heat of the day still lingered to the point where sweat prickled his skin as he sat on his balcony with his phone in his hand. Just like before, his stomach was a tangle of nerves as he worked up the courage to call Kiana.

But this time, it was for a different reason.

Before, he wasn't sure if the attraction was mutual, but the heat of their kiss this afternoon left no question about that. She wanted him as much as he wanted her. It was her behavior around her family that bothered him more now. How she could go from hot to cold so quickly. How she refused to make eye contact with him. How Tre's accusatory glare was as equally directed toward her as it was him.

And his gut told him it was better to get to the bottom of it now than be blindsided down the road.

He dialed her number and waited for her to pick up.

Just when he thought he was going to end up in voice mail purgatory, she picked up.

"Hello," she said in a voice barely above a whisper.

"Hey, lovely lady."

A sharp intake of breath answered him, followed by a long pause. "Let me move to another room."

He heard the muffled sound of her voice, followed by the soft shutting of a door, and his fingers twitched. Where was she? And what was she doing that she needed to step away to talk to him?

"Sorry about that, Frank," she said, still speaking in the same hushed tone. "Why are you calling so late?"

"It's not even nine." He forced himself to sound casual, even though his sweat production had doubled in less than a minute. "What are you doing?"

"I'm at home."

He was tempted to ask if she was alone, but he already knew the answer. Why else would she cover the phone and speak to someone else before stepping into another room? He rubbed his hand on his shirt and scratched the back of his head. "It's really nice down here in Orlando."

"Did you call just to gloat?"

"Maybe."

She responded with that low, sexy laugh of hers, and some of the tension fled his shoulders. "Is that all?"

He looked behind him at the big empty room and equally empty king-sized bed. In the past, he would've headed straight for the clubs to pick up some fun for the night, but right now, there was only one woman he wanted to share his space with. "Would you like to come down and join me?"

"Frank—"

He heard the note of rejection in her voice, but he cut her off and plowed ahead, desperate to sell her on the idea. "I'll even pay for a first-class ticket, Kiana. We could catch a few games, have some nice dinners, maybe even play in the amusement parks. And then, at the end of the day…"

He purposely left it hanging to let her fill in the blank. He already knew what he'd do if he had her with him.

Silence lingered on the line, and he offered a silent prayer that meant she was considering his offer. But when she spoke, he caught a hint of the conflict raging inside her. "It sounds wonderful—it really does—and I'd love to be able to join you, but I—" Her voice halted like she'd almost let something slip out and caught herself just in time. "I just can't."

The hairs on the back of his neck rose, and he stood up straighter. "Why not?"

"Because I can't."

"Give me a good reason why." He'd either learn the truth, or he'd win her to his side. Until then, he wasn't going to accept her answer.

"Frank…" She said his name like an exasperated sigh. "Unlike you, I have a job I have to go every day."

"But it's the weekend."

"That still doesn't change the fact that I have plans and appointments and other things that I can't brush aside."

He gritted his teeth, and the knots returned to his stomach. "What's so important that you can't get away for a few days?"

Another pause filled the line, and he curled his fingers

around the railing of the balcony.

"Please, Frank, between the foundation and my family, my schedule is full."

"So you can't make any time for me? Is that what you're saying?"

"No, I didn't say that," she snapped, and for the first time in this conversation, he felt the tide turning in his direction. "What I'm saying is that I'm not the spontaneous type, so if you want to do something, I need to know in advance so I can make arrangements."

Her explanation still didn't settle the suspicions forming in his mind. "Prove it."

"Why, you arrogant—"

He cut her off again, this time with a low chuckle. Somehow, he'd managed to rile her up as much as she had him. "Forgive me if I want to spend time with you, especially after our *meeting* this morning."

A secretive giggle answered him, and he could almost picture her cheeks flushing like they had when they'd almost gotten caught. "Fine. When are you coming back to Atlanta?"

"Don't know. Maybe at the end of the week." It was a dick move, but if she could play vague, so could he. Make her wonder what he was up to.

He hoped it would spark some flame of jealousy or possessiveness, but instead, all he got was a cool, collected voice accompanied by a few clicks of a mouse. "Would Friday work for you?" she asked as though she were scheduling him for a dental appointment rather than a hot date.

Damn the woman. She had him so turned around, he

wasn't sure which end was up. "Friday night would work, but only if it involved dinner. And dessert."

He said that last part in such a low, seductive way that there would be no doubt in her mind that she was what he planned on indulging in after the meal.

Her breath hitched, and he silently laughed. Maybe she would be game for skipping dinner and going straight for dessert if he was lucky.

A few more clicks followed, and that professional voice returned. "I have you tentatively penciled in for dinner on Friday night at seven."

Oh, sweet Jesus! Would he have to schedule sex with her, too? This was why he hated phone calls with women. It was always much easier to convince them to go along with his plans when he could exercise all his charms on them in person. But he wanted her so badly, he'd play along. "You sure you can't come down here sooner?"

"Sorry, Frank, but—" She dropped her voice to a whisper and finished. "But I look forward to Friday night."

There was just enough sexiness in her reply to keep him from listening to the warning bells going off in the back of his mind. "I'll make reservations for STK."

He'd wine her and dine her, just to prove to her he could be a gentleman. But after dinner, he made no promises.

"Deal." She hung up, giving him enough time to clear his mind and dissect the conversation.

The back-and-forth bothered him, but at least he'd managed to convince her to go out with him again. One thing became undeniably clear, though, from the hushed tones and hesitations.

She was hiding something from him.

He paced the balcony while his mind raced with possibilities. Maybe she was with another man. Shit, maybe she was married and was just using him to help her foundation. For a second, he was tempted to call Tre and find out, but based on the existing tension surrounding the two siblings, he didn't want to cause Kiana any more grief there.

He needed answers, and there was only one person he could turn to for them.

He dialed Adam's number.

"Please tell me you're not in jail or the hospital," his eldest brother answered as soon as he picked up.

"Cut me some slack, Adam."

"This is you we're talking about, Frank." The sound of women's voices filtered in over the line and grew more distant with each second, so different from the muffled, one-way conversation when Kiana answered. "Sorry, but Lia and I have Mom over for dinner. Now, what have you done, and how much is it going to cost me to bail you out?"

Frank rolled his eyes and stepped back in the air-conditioned hotel room. He was already getting enough heat from his brother. He didn't need the extra humidity. "It's not like that at all. I'm down in Orlando, alone, in my hotel room, working on business."

"Who are you, and what have you done with my brother?"

Easy laughter rolled up from the center of Frank's chest. "What's the matter, Adam? Not used to hearing that

I'm behaving?"

"Again, this is you we're talking about. But there must be something up for you to call me, and I have a suspicion it might have something to do with why you're alone on a Friday night."

"Bingo." Frank sat down at the desk and fired up his laptop. "I'm trying to figure out Kiana."

He did a Google search for her name and was surprised to find the picture of them at the Hawks game near the top of the list. The memory of that kiss sent the blood rushing from his head to his dick, and he slammed the laptop shut before it robbed him of all common sense. "I have a feeling she's withholding some important information from me."

"Such as?"

"That's what I want to find out." He jumped up from the desk and raked his fingers through his sweat-damp hair. "I know she was mixed up with that asshole I sent to the hospital, and from what I can gather, he hit her when they were together, but my gut tells me that's just the tip of the iceberg."

"All women have secrets," his brother said in a calm, matter-of-fact way.

"I know, but I can't shake the feeling she's got more than most women."

"And your reason for unearthing them would be...?"

Frank sank down on the edge of the bed and wished his stomach would stop churning. "I like her. A lot, actually. But I want to know what I'm getting myself into before I get in too deep, if you know what I mean, but I have no idea how to broach the subject."

"Hmmm…" A keyboard clicked on the other side of the line, and Adam said, "Looks like you have no problem locking lips with her in public."

He must've found the picture from the basketball game, too.

"Do you blame me?"

"I'm a married man, so I plead the Fifth."

Frank grinned. "Worried Lia might give you a hard time if you admit Kiana's hot?"

"Not when the woman in question obviously has a thing for my brother. Besides, I told you I like petite Italian women."

A feminine laugh came from the distance, and Frank could almost imagine his sister-in-law listening in on the conversation.

"But I'll contact Cully in the morning and see if I can get some answers for you," Adam continued.

"I don't think we need to go to that extreme. I just wanted some tips on how to bring it up without getting my face slapped."

"Just be honest, but not confrontational. If she sees you as a threat, she'll raise her defenses. I hope that helps. In the meantime, I think Mom wants to talk to you."

Frank groaned. He already had enough on his mind without his mother prying into his personal life. He hoped Adam had enough sense to hide the picture of him and Kiana at the game, but luck wasn't on his side tonight.

"Who's that lovely young woman you're seeing, Frank?" Mom asked, her voice full of matchmaking hope.

"One date, Mom. It was just one date."

"But she's stunning. And you two make such a

95

handsome couple."

I need to smack Adam on the back of the head next time I see him. He bet Mom was already planning his wedding.

"Her name's Kiana," he answered, giving his mom as little information as possible.

"And what does she do?"

"She manages a charity foundation."

"Oh, like Becca?"

Frank bit back a bitter laugh. Ethan's girlfriend ran a foundation, too, but it was entirely different from what Kiana dealt with on a daily basis. Becca had it easy. She had her family's fortune at her disposal. Kiana was out in the trenches trying to raise money to help the kids who benefitted from her hard work. "Not exactly."

"Still, that's a much better occupation than some of the other women you've dated."

Frank silently cursed. Had his mother been spying on him? "Yes, Mom. She's a nice young woman from a respectable family here in Atlanta."

"You've met her family?" He could almost hear her asking why she hadn't met Kiana yet.

"I'm friends with her brother. And it was just one date." This conversation was growing more awkward by the minute. He was going to kill Adam.

"Well, it looks like you two hit it off."

Frank flopped back on the bed and flung his arm over his eyes. His face burned. "It was for the Kiss Cam, Mom."

"Isn't that the excuse Ben gave for the night he met Hailey?"

What his mom meant to ask was if his evening ended

the same way his brother's had. "Mom, I did not take her back to my place."

Of course, if he'd had his way, his evening would've gone exactly like Ben's had, ending with some unforgettable sex. The only difference would be that he'd make sure to wear two condoms. He was way too young to be saddled with a kid.

"Oh, really?" His mother actually sounded disappointed. The woman wanted grandkids so badly, she didn't care how she got them. She'd made a huge fuss over Jenny's baby, and it wasn't even Dan's. He only hoped it would ease up once his brothers gave her what she wanted.

"Mom, can we please stop talking about my personal life?"

"Very well," she said with a heavy dose of resignation. "Have you been staying out of trouble?"

"Yes, Mom, I've been a good boy. I'm even down in Orlando for some charity work."

"And would this charity be in any way related to Kiana?"

His mother was too smart for her own good. "Yes, Mom."

"You'll have to tell me more about it."

"Maybe later. It's late, and I have some early meetings in the morning," he lied, using the excuse Kiana had given him the night of the game.

"Are you sure you're feeling okay, Frank?"

He wanted to tell his mother about the odd ache in his gut and the way his breath quickened whenever he was around Kiana, but it felt too personal, especially when he wasn't quite sure what to make of it himself. "Yeah, I'm fine. Why?"

"I'm just not used to you acting so...um, responsible."

Everyone was a comedian, especially when it came to picking on him. "Would you prefer I revert to my old ways?"

"No, no, no. I'm just very proud of you, dear, that's all. You're finally growing up into the fine young man I always knew you'd be."

"As opposed to the screw-up I was before?"

"I'd never say a three-time Pro-Bowler was a screw-up, dear."

His lips twitched into a half-smile. Mom always knew how to make him feel better. "Just trying to make you proud."

"You always have. And I hope to hear more about this young lady you're seeing. Maybe I can plan a little trip down to Atlanta in a few weeks. I'll even bring Jasper with me."

"Hold on a minute, Mom. Let's take things one step at a time. I need to make it to a second date first." And he definitely didn't need his mother's big, slobbering dog shedding all over his place if he wanted to have a chance of convincing Kiana to stay the night.

"But he's such an excellent judge of character."

"Chill, Mom." Frank rubbed his chin, though, as he thought about it. Maybe the Jasper test would be faster than waiting to get the truth from her.

"Yes, dear. In the meantime, you get some rest, and don't forget to give me a call every now and then."

Ugh! The guilt. He'd forgotten how good his mother

was at dishing it out. "Yes, Mom."

He hung up before his family found something else to tease him about and stretched out on the bed. Life would've been so much easier if Kiana had just accepted his invitation. Instead, he was left hanging in the balance and unsure of what he needed to do next.

***

Kiana hung up the phone after accepting Frank's dinner invitation and fanned her flushed face. She'd just started getting Savannah ready for bed when he'd called, and she'd been so scared her daughter would start wailing in the background. But her fears were unfounded, as Savannah had remained perfectly silent after she'd slipped out of the nursery.

Maybe it was time to tell him about her daughter. Before she got in over her head. Denise had said to listen to her heart and her gut, but it was her raging hormones that were driving her decisions right now. And all her hormones told her to get at least one night of pleasure from Frank before dropping the bomb on him.

She typed out a quick text message to Madison, asking if she would mind staying a little later on Friday. If her nanny couldn't, she'd turn to Sherita or Denise for baby-sitting duty. Luckily, though, Madison replied in less than a minute that she could.

One hurdle down. Now, picking out something nice to wear.

She peeked into the nursery and found Savannah playing in her crib. As soon as her daughter saw her, she stood up, arms extended, and said, "Mama."

Kiana's heart melted the same way it did every time she

saw her little girl. The precious child had helped her make hard decisions in the past, so there was no question where she stood on the list of Kiana's priorities. No man was worth risking her daughter's safety and well-being.

As she picked Savannah up and carried her to her bedroom, she wondered where Frank would fit into their family. He'd already proven that he had a white knight complex when he'd come to her rescue that night in the club, and he'd shown more restraint than any other man she'd dated.

But Tre's words still haunted her. Frank seemed to lack a serious bone in his body, and yet he'd shown more than his fair share of responsibility for his part in the fundraiser. How would he react if she told him about Savannah?

She rubbed her hand over her daughter's soft curls and asked, "So what should Mommy wear to dinner?"

Savannah blew her a drool-covered raspberry.

Kiana grinned and set the toddler down at her favorite place in the closet—the shoe rack—and typed out one more quick text message.

Looking forward to dinner next week.

A minute later, Frank replied back, *Me too, lovely lady.*

Her heart melted again, but this time, for an entirely different reason.

Savannah had already grabbed a stiletto and was trying to slip her tiny foot into it when Kiana looked down. "Starting the addiction early, I see," she teased the toddler.

Then she made her way down the row of dresses hanging in the closet. "So, Savannah, should Mommy go for naughty or nice?"

Savannah replied by grabbing a sparkling silver strappy

sandal with six-inch heels and offering it up to her.

Kiana took it as a sign. "Naughty it is, then."

Chapter Nine

Frank Kelly sat alone in a booth at one of the best steakhouses in Atlanta on Friday night and stared at his phone.

7:25 PM.

And no sign of Kiana.

He'd only touched base with her once since he'd called last week because he was afraid he might let it slip that he was having her investigated. But in that brief conversation, no matter how many times he'd offered to pick her up, she'd insisted on meeting him at the restaurant.

Which, of course, set off his spidey sense once again that she was hiding something from him.

And now she was standing him up.

He tried calling her for the third time that evening, but like the other times before, it went straight to voice mail. Any other guy would've read that as a loud and clear sign she wasn't interested, but when he clicked on her info, he saw the text message she'd sent him when he was in Orlando.

Looking forward to dinner next week.

He turned off his phone and flagged the server for his check. It was only for a drink, but there was no reason to tie up the table any longer. He left a generous tip as an apology and went to the one place he stood any chance of getting answers.

Her office.

***

Kiana was on hold.

Again.

She tapped her foot on the floor and raked her fingers through her hair while she listened to bland music on the other end of the line. She'd been on the phone all afternoon after learning they'd sold more tickets for the gala than they'd planned. That meant getting a bigger space. And bringing in more liquor. And now, trying to get an estimate from the caterer on the food. And they all put her on hold when she asked for a number.

It was enough to make her want to pull her hair out.

She glanced up at the dress hanging from her file cabinet. At least she had something to look forward to once she got through this last phone call. She'd been waiting all week for dinner with Frank, and the form-fitting, sequined gown was a perfect mix of naughty and nice. Not to mention, it went perfectly with the shoes Savannah had recommended.

A woman with a deep Southern drawl finally came on the line. "Yeah, we can feed that many people, but it will double your quote."

"But this is a charity event, Miss Rosa."

"And I have a business to run," the woman answered.

Time to play hardball. "A business that rose to prominence because my daddy endorsed it when you were just starting out."

Miss Rosa didn't reply immediately, and Kiana took advantage of the woman's hesitation. "This foundation was my daddy's dream, and I'm doing my best to keep it alive. I'm over the moon that the anticipated attendance for the gala has doubled, but I want to keep as much money as I can for the kids. Please, can you give me a little discount? If not for the foundation, then at least as a thank-you for all my daddy did for you when he was alive?"

Some muted grumbles filled the line, followed by the drone of sedating music.

Shit! On hold again.

This time, however, it only lasted for a couple of minutes. "If I give you a ten percent discount, will you provide me with a receipt so I can claim it as a tax deduction?" Miss Rosa countered.

Kiana nearly jumped out of her chair. "Deal!"

"I'm already cutting you a better deal than most of my clients, after all, and this is a last-minute adjustment."

"I know, Miss Rosa, and thank you so much for accommodating all the extra guests. Thank you, thank you."

"One more thing." Miss Rosa lowered her voice and added, "My boy is a huge fan of Frank Kelly, and his birthday is coming up. If you could get him to sign something for him—"

"Consider it done." It shouldn't be too hard to convince Frank to sign a football or a jersey for a teenage boy.

"Thank you, Kiana." The caterer hung up, and Kiana sprang from her desk to change for dinner.

Night had fallen over Atlanta, and the skyscrapers glittered on the horizon. The clear weather came at a cost. A cold front had moved through this morning, and the temperature had dropped over thirty degrees from when she left the house. Suddenly, those strappy sandals didn't look so appealing. But it would all be worth it when she saw the look on Frank's face.

The dress dated back to before she'd gotten pregnant, thus requiring her heavy-duty Spanx. There was no way she'd ever come close to getting her pre-baby body back without the use of the constrictive Lycra undergarment. She tugged at the high-waisted shorts for several minutes before she squeezed all of her generous curves inside, sweat prickling along her forehead. But once the dress slipped on over the Spanx, the effort was worth it.

She applied some smoky eye shadow to her light brown eyes and a burgundy shade of lipstick that was far too daring for the day job, but perfect for a night out. Once the makeup was set, she reached for her shoes and sat down on the small sofa in her office to strap them on.

She was in process of buckling the second one when she heard a knock.

Frank filled the doorway, his tie hanging loosely around his neck like he'd started to take it off. The dark blue suit complemented his eyes, but the perturbed expression on his face captured her attention and made her heart lurch. "It's a little late for that," he said and pointed to the clock on the wall behind her desk.

7:52 PM.

Shit!

An icy river of dread filled her veins, and her explanation stumbled forth. "Frank, I'm so sorry. I just lost track of the time. I—"

The words froze on her tongue as he stepped toward her. Memories of how Malcolm would find any excuse to hit her overrode everything she knew about Frank. All she saw was a big, hulking man who had every reason to be angry with her. One who could easily beat the crap out of her for this.

She curled up into a little ball on the sofa and kept repeating, "I'm sorry, I'm sorry."

He stopped short, and his brows gathered together. "Kiana, what's wrong?"

"I'm sorry I forgot about dinner. It won't happen again. I was just on the phone with the caterer, and—"

"That's not what I'm talking about." He reached for her, and she instinctively jerked back against the sofa. His arm fell slack, followed by the expression on his face. "Jesus, Kiana, what did that bastard do to you?"

And just like that, the present came crashing into focus, and tears prickled her eyes. "I'm sorry, Frank."

"Stop saying that." He turned around and raked his fingers through his hair with a loud exhalation. "Just tell me what happened. And no more apologies."

Her body trembled, but she couldn't tell if it was from fear or relief. Or maybe just embarrassment. She'd automatically thought the worst of him, and now shame scorched her skin. "We've sold so many tickets for the gala that we exceeded our expectations. I've been on the

106

phone all day to make sure we had enough room and food and drinks for the attendees."

"So that's why you didn't answer your phone?" he asked, his back still to her.

She nodded, even though she knew he couldn't see her. "I was on the phone with the caterer until about ten minutes ago."

He put his hands on his hips and stared out of her office window. "And that's why you stood me up."

"I didn't mean to. I just lost track of time, and..." The implication behind his comment finally hit her. He'd been waiting for her at the restaurant, and she'd never shown up. And after she'd turned him down on the Orlando trip, who knew what he'd been thinking? "Oh, shit, Frank, I'm so sorry."

"Stop apologizing." He turned around and rubbed his hand along the side of his face. "These things can't be helped."

She finally felt safe enough to allow her legs to uncurl, but she didn't trust them enough to rise from the sofa. "Is it too late for dinner?"

"It is for STK." His eyes flickered over her body, stopping at the plunging neckline that exposed a generous amount of cleavage. "You look nice, by the way."

Her cheeks warmed, but for an entirely different reason now. "We can still go out, if you want."

"My place is always open." He flashed a seductive grin that almost had her agreeing to his suggestion.

But her reaction to him moments ago tempered her enthusiasm. She still didn't trust him. Not completely. Not yet. And definitely not enough to follow him back to his place. She shook her head. "Nope. Too far, and I have a curfew tonight."

Or at least, she'd promised Madison she'd be home by eleven.

"Fine," he said with an exaggerated pout. "Time for plan B."

He tossed his phone to her and went around her desk. "There's an app for a local pizza place on there. Order whatever you want and have them deliver it here."

She held his phone, but didn't follow his instructions right away. "What are you planning?"

"Dinner and a movie." He typed a few things on her keyboard and flipped her monitor around to reveal the webpage for a site that streamed movies. "You sound like you could use a breather, and I can only bear to wear this necktie for so long."

In other words, he was trying to meet her on her turf, to leave her in control of the evening. His actions tore down her defenses and thawed the remaining fear that still lingered in her blood. She couldn't have asked for a more perfect plan B. "Thank you, Frank."

"I like the sound of that much better than an apology." He gave her a hopeful smile. "Now order that pizza, and when you're done, pick out a movie."

She found the app and looked at the menu. "What kind of pizza do you like?"

"Your call. If it's pizza, I'll eat it." He started to shrug and paused. "Except no tofu. I draw the line at fake meat."

And for the first time that evening, she felt comfortable enough to laugh. "Me, too."

He met her gaze, and his smile widened.

Her heart gave a little flip-flop. Frank was so different from Malcolm. Her ex would've had her bleeding on the floor for missing a dinner date—especially at a place as nice as STK—but Frank just rolled with the punches and came up with something new. There was an easy-goingness to him that calmed her frazzled nerves. He was big. And yes, he knew how to throw a punch. But she was finally beginning to see she was safe with him.

"Are you going to order?" he asked, interrupting her thoughts. "Because I'm starving."

"Of course. I mean, I bet you are after waiting at the restaurant for so long. I'm truly s—"

"I thought I said no more apologies." There was a stern quality to his voice that silenced her, but the twinkle in his eyes softened the harshness of his words. "You got wrapped up at work. I get it."

"Do you?"

He glanced down at the floor and scratched the back of his head. "Yeah, I do. I mean, I feel the same way about my job. But I'd be lying if I said I wasn't a little bit jealous."

At that, her guard went up, and her muscles tensed. "Jealous of what?"

He gave a self-deprecating laugh and nudged the toe of his shoe against her desk. "I just wish there was a way I could capture your attention as much as your job did."

And once again, she was back to melting on the inside. He might not have known it, but he'd said just the right thing. "Well, you have my complete attention tonight. Or least until 10:45."

"Hey, even Cinderella had until midnight."

She ordered a large pizza with all the meats and a two-liter soda while using the time to collect her thoughts. This was her chance to tell him about Savannah. But she'd already pressed her luck too much tonight. Telling him about her kid might be the deal-breaker. No, it was better to take things slowly and see where they went first. "Cinderella didn't have a nine AM interview with the local TV network the following morning. I need my beauty rest."

"I don't know." He came around the desk and leaned on the edge. "You look pretty beautiful to me."

"And you don't know how much goes into looking like this." She finalized the order, not at all surprised to find Frank had stored a credit card number on the account with the pizza place. "You need to secure your personal information better."

"They have to guess my password first. Now, pick out the movie." He tapped her computer screen.

"Are you sure you don't want to fill me in on how your trip to Orlando went?"

He shook his head. "You've been working too much. It's now time to play. Dinner. Movie. Business can wait until Monday."

"Fine." When she stood, her knees only gave the slightest of wobbles, but she blamed that more on the unfastened sandal strap rather than the dread from earlier. She leaned over to grab the mouse from the other side of the desk.

"Nice view from here," Frank quipped, his gaze firmly fixed on her backside.

She laughed again and gave him a little wiggle to see if he'd grab the way he had the night of the basketball game, but his arms remained firmly crossed over his chest. Almost restrained across his chest, to be more accurate. It was like the other night when he'd promised not to lay a hand on her.

Maybe he read her better than she thought. It was obvious that he wanted to touch her, but after her meltdown, he was probably giving her space and waiting for her to give him the green light.

And one more wall came crashing down around her heart. At the rate he was going, Frank Kelly was well on his way to winning it.

She scrolled through the movies on the streaming service, unsure of what to pick. Then she switched over to the recently viewed tab and was greeted by a list of comedies with the rare action film dotted in. Yeah, it was pure Frank. A man who liked to laugh, not see people beat the pulp out of each other. She worked her way down the list until she found something she liked. "How 'bout we go a little retro?"

She clicked on the movie, and a few seconds later, a title with a skull and crossbones filled her computer screen.

"*The Goonies!*" Frank exclaimed like an overly excited kid. "Absolutely one of the best movies ever."

"Yeah, it's pretty good."

"Pretty good?" He looked at her like she'd lost her mind. "This movie is a classic. Come on—I'll show you."

He took her hand and led her back to the sofa. "Wait a minute. I don't need this." He shrugged off his jacket. "Or

111

this." He yanked off his tie.

Then he scooped her up in his arms and flopped back on the sofa so she was seated in his lap. "And you don't need these," he finished, slipping off her sparkling stiletto sandals.

She rested her hands on his shoulders and grinned. "You really are something else, Frank Kelly."

"You're just now realizing that?"

"I've seen bits and pieces here and there, but it's all starting to come together."

"Good." He took her right hand and lowered it to his chest until it rested over his heart. "Because I have every intention of making you smile tonight."

A rebellious jolt of desire shot to her lower pelvis. There was definitely one way he could make her smile. Too bad the pizza guy could walk in on them at any moment.

His grin widened as though he knew exactly what she was thinking. And judging by the hard bulge pressing into her bottom, he was feeling something similar, too. He slid her off his lap to the seat next to him. "But first, I need to prove to you that *The Goonies* is a cinematic masterpiece."

CHAPTER TEN

God, it was a night of the most exquisite torture he'd ever known.

Kiana's soft, sexy laugh.

Her warm curves pressed up against him.

The intoxicating perfume that clung to her skin.

It was enough to have him sweating out the date like he was back in high school and wondering when he should make the move to first base. Or even beyond, if he was lucky.

But every time he thought about touching her, he flashed back on the way she'd cowered on the very same sofa she was calmly sitting on now. Her repeated apologies haunted him. Jesus, what had the bastard done to her? Based on her behavior, her ex must have roughed her up pretty badly for being late for dinner. It was enough to caution him to cool his jets, even though all he wanted to do was wrap his arms around her and hold her until her fears vanished.

He meant what he said about wanting to make her

smile, and based on her relaxed posture and easy grin, he was succeeding. Not in the way he'd intended, but he'd take it.

Thankfully, he'd seen *The Goonies* more times than he could count. That left the evening open to learning all he could about Kiana and how to read her emotions. He spent most of the movie watching her and memorizing every little detail he could. For example, she glanced down when she laughed. She pursed her lips together while twirling a curl around her finger when she seemed to be concentrating on something. And she laced her fingers together and brought them up to her lips when things got tense. All things he filed away for later.

But when the credits starting rolling on the screen, he was paralyzed about what to do next.

"Fair enough, Frank," she said with another one of those soft laughs that doubled the blood flow to his dick. "That was a fun movie."

"Told you so."

"Wait a minute." She turned toward him, her thighs pressing against his. "I said it was fun. I'm not so sure about it being a cinematic masterpiece."

"Perhaps we need to watch it again to convince you otherwise."

For the first time that evening, she looked up when she laughed.

He took that as a sign that she'd finally recovered from her earlier fright, and he leaned in closer, dropping his voice to a seductive rumble. "Or did you have something else in mind?"

Her breath caught, and he silently cursed. *Way to screw it up for being too hot to trot.*

But she didn't back away. Instead, she stared at him and licked her lips like he was some decadent treat she was dying to devour.

If she'd been any other woman, he'd take that as an invitation to lock his lips with hers until she begged him to fuck her senseless. But since it was Kiana, he forced himself to hold back. Hell, he even refused to touch her. The last thing he wanted to become in her eyes was an oppressive, domineering asshole. He'd put the ball in her court, and he was going to let her decide how far she wanted to go.

He didn't have to wait long. She closed the gap between them and pressed her full lips to his. He closed his eyes and lost himself in the sweet bliss of her kiss.

But as the kiss grew more demanding, he found himself caught in the agony of desire. He balled his hands into fists, determined not to lay a hand on her without her permission even though the only thing he wanted to do was cradle every delicious curve of her body.

She stopped and pulled away. "Is something wrong?"

He kept his eyes shut because if he even had the slightest of glimpses of her kiss-swollen lips, he'd be in danger of crossing the line. Instead, he merely nodded and tried to ignore the ache in his groin.

"Trying to be a good boy?"

He nodded again. *Shit, this fucking hurt.*

Her breath bathed his ear, increasing the pounding in his dick. "Don't be."

And with those two words, she'd given him all the permission he needed. He grabbed her ass and pulled her toward him until her knees straddled his lap. Then he kissed her like he'd wanted to do since the moment he'd seen her in that ridiculously tiny dress. He'd used up all his gentleness for the evening. All he had left was the raw lust pulsating through his veins.

He crushed his lips to hers and didn't bother pleading with her to open her mouth. Not that he needed to. She readily gave him access to it and met him head on. He likened it to running into a wall of offensive linemen and maneuvering past their defenses to sack the quarterback. Only Kiana wasn't fighting to hold him back. She was fighting him for dominance.

She bunched the collar of his shirt in her fists while her tongue did all kinds of naughty things to his mouth. He made the mistake of imagining what it would be like if she was doing those things to his dick, and that piece of anatomy grew so hard, it strained against his zipper. A groan rose up from the center of his chest, and he squeezed her ass even harder to keep from losing his mind. "Damn it, Kiana, you have no idea how sexy you are."

"Right back at ya, Romeo."

He would've been upset that she chose to bring up his nickname if she hadn't softened the blow by grinding against him in a lap dance that set every nerve below the belt on edge. When she started unbuttoning his shirt, he got the message loud and clear. He'd been given permission to go past first base.

He followed her lead and massaged his way up her back until his hands closed around the zipper holding her dress together. In one fluid motion, he slid it down, and her dress fell down to her waist.

He finally felt brave enough to open his eyes, and when he did, his breath hitched. The sheer black lace bra gave him more than an eyeful of her perfectly round breasts. He cupped one overflowing mound in his hand and ran his thumb over the dark peak in the center.

Now it was her turn to moan.

He liked the sound of it. He wanted her to want him as much as he wanted her. He wanted to know what she liked and disliked. He wanted to push all the right buttons, just as she had done so far tonight with him. And when neither of them could hold back any longer, he knew the sex would be beyond anything he'd ever experienced before.

Because this time, it would be different. Instead of banging some girl he barely knew, he was holding on to a woman who captivated his mind and his senses outside the bedroom. She was someone he could sleep with and still have a great conversation with the next day. And that heightened the anticipation even more for him.

She shoved his shirt down past his shoulders, jerking his hand away from her breast, but he used her impatience to his advantage. The action brought his lips closer to that tantalizing peak, and he caught it between his teeth.

She dug her nails into his triceps and said his name in a low, husky voice that oozed pure sex.

Yep, something she definitely liked.

He drew her nipple into his mouth and swirled his tongue around it, the rough edges of the lace contrasting with the silky skin underneath. She tasted just as delicious as he knew she would. With a few well-practiced maneuvers, he unhooked her bra and tossed it across the room, leaving nothing between his mouth and her.

Her breaths grew ragged, but she made no move to push him away. Instead, she threaded her fingers through his hair and held him there, arching her back to give him full access to her breasts. When he caught a hint of a whimper in her voice, he switched sides and repeated it all over again.

After a few minutes, something shifted in her behavior. Her cries became more desperate, just like the frantic way her hips moved over his lap. "Please tell me you have a condom."

He released her breast long enough to reply, "In my jacket."

She caught his cheeks in her hands and kissed him so hard, it seemed to ask what he was waiting for.

He blindly reached for the jacket he'd draped over the side of the sofa earlier, only to find it had been knocked to the floor during their foreplay. A curse flew from his lips as he ended the kiss long enough to retrieve it.

In the meantime, Kiana went to work on his belt, whipping it off in a matter of seconds. Her eagerness matched his own, but when she wrapped her hands around his dick, he lost all coherent thoughts.

Holy Mary, mother of God, that felt good.

He could sit there all day and let her stroke her warm hands up and down the length of his cock.

"Frank?" she asked, ripping him from his fantasies and reminding him of what he had right in front of him "The condom?"

He fumbled for his jacket, his movements as clumsy

and frantic as a guy about to get laid for the first time. Another whispered curse escaped. Not the way he wanted her to picture him. He wanted to be smooth, suave, experienced. He wanted to live up to her expectations and carry out his promise of making her come.

His hand closed around the foil packet, and he held it up for her. "Found it."

"Good." She snatched it from his hand and ripped open the package. A second later, she had rolled it down his entire length and was tugging his pants past his knees, all while capturing his mouth in the most erotic kiss he'd ever experienced.

Perhaps he should return the favor. He reached up her skirt, expecting to find little lacy panties that matched her bra, only to come in contact with an industrial-strength material that refused to budge. "Shit! How do you get these off?"

"With a crowbar," she teased.

"Kind of prevents us from going any further, don't you think?"

That sexy laugh answered him, and she raised her hips. "It's time you learned the secret of the Spanx."

She lowered herself onto his lap, and the next thing he knew, he was buried deep inside her.

Damn! It was even better than he imagined. So hot. So wet. So tight that he was in danger of coming right there. The only thing that held him back was the sheer impossibility of it all. "How?"

"There's a slit opening." She rocked back on her hips, sending little waves of pleasure rippling along his dick. "Now shut up and fuck me."

"Yes, ma'am." It was one command he was more than happy to comply with. Especially when being inside her felt this good. And just as her hands and her tongue promised, she knew exactly how to bring him to the edge. Up and down, back and forth, she rode him like a woman who knew what she wanted and how to get it.

And he let her. His hands only offered minimum guidance as they rested on her hips, and his lips were far too occupied tasting the skin along her neck and shoulders to say anything else. He wasn't used to not being in control. With other women, he controlled the tempo. With his last few lays, he'd gone fast and furious, focused on coming as quickly as he could once he'd charmed them into his bed. Then, once he was done, he'd move on to the next woman since none of them held his interest after the hookup.

But he wasn't in a hurry now. If he could, he'd become an expert in tantric sex just so he could spend as much time buried inside Kiana. As it was, she knew how to draw it out and heighten each sensation until it bordered on pain. But damn, what a sweet way to be tortured.

She pressed her fingers into the muscles of his shoulders, and her hips returned to that same frantic pace from earlier. When she said his name, it came out like a plea for help.

And he was more than willing to give it to her if it meant sending her over the edge. He'd promised to make her come, and damn it, he refused to disappoint her.

He tightened his hold on her hips, taking over the rhythm. The long, fluid strokes turned into sharp jabs that produced equally sharp cries from her. The expression on her face, though, hardly spoke of pain. The tense line of her mouth, the flare of her nostrils, the heat in her eyes—they all belonged to a woman so close to orgasm that she was waiting for the moment when he hit the spot that sent her over the edge.

If only he wasn't so close to the edge himself. She was so fucking beautiful, he couldn't take his eyes off her. Combined with the way her inner walls tightened around his dick with every stroke, he was breaking out in a sweat just from holding back. His balls ached from the intensity of it all, and just when he thought he was done for, she cried out his name once more and tensed in his arms. She squeezed around him as he gave her one final thrust and followed her into the reckless abandon of ecstasy.

His senses blurred, and the only thing he was aware of was the pulsating pleasure that rolled through him. Damn, that felt so good. Too good. If he didn't know any better, Kiana and her Spanx had ruined him. He'd never imagined sex through a slit in granny panties would be so fucking amazing.

But as the world came back into focus, he discovered one of them was trembling. At first, he thought it was her, but much to his shock, it was him. His body shook from the intensity of the aftershock still radiating through him. He pressed his forehead against hers and struggled to catch his breath. "Never take those panties off. Ever."

Her low laughter answered him, and she ran her fingers through his hair and along his face. "So you're saying you weren't turned off by the Spanx."

"Fuck no." He grabbed her ass and pressed her hard against him. "And as soon as I'm recovered, I'll be ready for round two."

"What makes you think there's going to be a round two?" she teased.

A brief flash of fear shot through him, only to be dissipated by the scorching hot kiss that spoke of rounds three and four. He relaxed and soaked it all in, massaging tiny circles into the small of her back with his thumbs. Kiana had enjoyed it as much as he had, and just like he suspected, they were more than compatible in the bedroom.

But as the kiss took on a tender note, a new fear rose inside him. Everything was so perfect right now that he was in serious danger of falling for her. But if she didn't feel the same about him…

I'm so in over my head.

But as long as she was in his arms, he didn't care.

Then the ringing of a cell phone came and ruined everything.

Kiana stiffened in his arms, her lips frozen against him with the first ring. By the second ring, she was bolting from his lap and reaching for it. She didn't even bother to look at the caller ID before answering. "What's wrong?"

She impatiently pulled her dress back up over her boobs as she listened to the person on the other end. "Slow down."

Frank sat paralyzed on the sofa, unable to process the sudden change in her behavior. All he could do was sit and watch as she searched the office for her bra with her phone pressed against her ear.

"No, you did the right thing. Where are you now?"

She found her bra and put it on in record time while

using her shoulder to hold the phone in place.

"Yes, that's fine. I'll be there as soon as I can." She hung up and turned back to him, her expression stark with panic as she zipped up her dress.

The first thing that popped into his mind was that her ex was threatening her. "What's wrong?"

She opened her mouth, but no sound came out. Then she closed it and grabbed the sensible shoes she'd probably worn earlier that day. "I'll tell you later."

"Can I do anything to help?"

Her head snapped up, and uncertainty wavered across her face. Then she lowered her eyes. "No, not right now. I just need to go."

She finished putting on her shoes, but he managed to get his pants up in time to catch her before she dashed out of the office. "Kiana, please, you look like you need help."

"I don't need any help," she replied, jerking away from him.

"You're the one who said you have a hard time asking for help, and well..." Her defiant glare told him he was getting nowhere with her. "I'm here for you if you need me."

Her expression softened. "Thank you, Frank." She stumbled back a step and added, "I'll call you tomorrow."

It wasn't the answer he wanted to hear, but it was better than having her shut him out completely. "Sooner, if you need to."

She nodded and ran out of the office, leaving him alone with his doubts. Who had called her? And why was she being so secretive about it all?

He sank down on the sofa where he'd been on cloud

nine moments ago and rubbed his chin. What a shitty way to end the evening. Just when he thought he'd finally broken down her walls, she'd pushed him away. And her actions only confirmed what he feared.

She was hiding something.

If he hadn't been suffering from sex hangover, he would've followed her down to the garage and to where she was going. He would've proven to her that he wouldn't be dismissed so easily. And he would've shown her that he was there for her when she needed him.

Instead, all he was left with was an ache in the center of his chest and a nagging suspicion that the truth would come crashing down around him sooner rather than later.

And after it did, would he be willing to keep fighting for her?

CHAPTER ELEVEN

The frantic pace of Kiana's heart was matched only by her footsteps as she raced through Egleston Children's Hospital to the ER. She'd known the moment she heard Madison's ringtone that something was wrong with her daughter. The nanny never bothered her unless there was. But her fear quadrupled when she heard the news.

Savannah had suffered an asthma attack that hadn't responded to her normal inhalers, and it had gotten so bad that Madison called 911. When the medics arrived, they'd recommended immediate transport, and they were in the process of loading her into the ambulance when the nanny had called her.

Kiana offered up the same prayer she'd been silently reciting since she'd left her office. *Dear Lord, please let her be okay.*

She didn't stop until she reached the reception desk of the ER and said in a breathless rush, "I'm Kiana Dyer. My daughter, Savannah, was brought by ambulance here."

"Let me check," the woman replied in a slow, easy

drawl.

Kiana resisted the urge to reach across the desk and shake the woman. Her daughter's life was in danger, and the damned receptionist failed to grasp how urgent the matter was. She cursed and pulled out her driver's license. "Here's my ID. It should match the address where she came from."

The receptionist looked at it and clicked her mouse several times before nodding. "Thank you, Ms. Dyer. Let me call the nurse to take you back to her."

Kiana squeezed her hands into fists to resist falling into a full-blown hissy fit right there in the waiting room. Luckily, a nurse appeared after a minute and waved her back.

"How's my daughter?" Kiana asked.

"A little better," the nurse replied. "We've gotten some steroids on board, and she's on a continuous neb. I'm sorry about the wait, but when a patient is on the Do Not Announce list, it requires a few extra steps to ensure her privacy."

Kiana drew in a long breath and nodded. How could she have forgotten that she'd registered Savannah on the Do Not Announce list? She'd done it so people like Malcolm wouldn't know where her daughter was. But the privacy came at the cost of those few precious moments.

The nurse led her to a room where Madison was holding Savannah in her lap while reading a story to her. A mask with an elephant on it covered her daughter's mouth and nose, and a fine mist escaped from the edges.

As soon as Savannah spotted her, she raised up her arms and said, "Mama."

Kiana pulled her daughter into her arms and hugged her tightly. "Hey, baby girl."

Savannah's breaths were rapid and shallow, each one accentuating her ribs underneath the thin hospital gown. The buzz of the nebulizer machine filled the room, drowning out the faint wheezes that vibrated through her chest. Kiana's heart ached from watching her little girl struggle to breathe, but she also considered herself blessed that her daughter was still breathing.

"Thank you, Madison, for your quick thinking."

"More like panic." The nanny hopped out of the chair so Kiana could sit. "I noticed she'd started to wheeze a little as the temperature dropped, so I gave her a few puffs of her inhaler, and she seemed fine until I tried to put her to bed. It just got so bad so quickly…"

Kiana closed her eyes and sat on the edge of the chair, still clinging to Savannah. Her daughter's first asthma attack had been like that, too, only at the time, she didn't have any inhalers. In less than half an hour, Savannah had gone from a happy infant to a baby gasping for air. After an intense ambulance ride, her daughter had spent five days in the hospital. How long would she be in this time?

"What have they done so far?" she asked, trying to drive out the fears gathering in the center of her chest.

"Gave her some medicine by mouth, swabbed her nose, and started this."

Sounded like last time. The first attack had been due to a virus called RSV, according to the doctors. Could this be the same thing?

"I've got her from here." She opened her eyes and gave Madison a weak smile. "Why don't you go on home and get some rest. I'll send you some updates when I have them."

"Please do." Madison gathered her coat and purse before ruffling Savannah's curls. "You gave me quite a scare there, sweetie, but you'd better be nicer to your mommy."

Savannah grinned at her through the nebulizer mask and waved bye-bye.

The wheezing improved enough over the next ten minutes to where Kiana felt comfortable enough to place her daughter in the crib and call Denise. When her stepmother answered, she said, "Sorry to wake you, Mama, but Savannah's in the ER with another one of her asthma attacks."

"I'll be there as soon as I can. Egleston?"

"Yes." She gave Denise the room number and reminded her to bring a picture ID.

Denise hung up before she could get another word in.

Kiana dragged her chair over to the crib and rested her forehead against the railing. She hated asking for help, but she was already drained from the day. First the changes to the gala. Then her evening with Frank. And the sex. God, the sex. It was spontaneous and reckless and...

And really fucking good.

Before she had a chance to question her actions, the doctor came into the room. She looked to be Kiana's age—way too young to be a doctor, yet the badge hanging from her lanyard had an "MD" on it. She introduced herself and came over to the crib with a smile. "Much better."

Savannah pulled herself up and reached for her mother.

128

Kiana lifted her out of the crib and placed her on her lap. "Did any of the labs come back?"

"All negative. I'm guessing it was the change in the weather, but she did have a little bit of a runny nose when I first saw her." The doctor stopped the nebulizer and removed the mask before listening to Savannah's lungs. "Yes, so much better."

Just the thing Kiana wanted to hear. "Can we go home now?"

"No, I want to observe her for a few hours, if that's all right with you. Your nanny said that Savannah had responded to her inhaler earlier today before worsening, and I want to make sure she isn't going to relapse once you get home. But for now, let's keep the fluids coming and see how she does. Are you fine with giving her some juice?"

Kiana nodded, another wave of weariness assaulting her. "She likes apple juice. And please dilute it with some water."

"Of course." The ER doc gave her a warm smile before leaving the room.

A few minutes later, a nurse appeared with a sippy cup of juice, which Savannah grabbed as soon as it came within her reach. The toddler sucked down the juice, choking a few times in the process. She was still breathing faster than normal, but otherwise, she appeared to be back to her usual self.

The nurse lingered to record Savannah's heart rate and oxygen levels. "Looking good, precious."

Another half hour crawled by before Denise arrived. "You poor baby girl."

Kiana didn't know if she was referring to her or Savannah, but it didn't matter. Denise was always there when she needed her. "Thank you for coming."

"Of course. Thank you for letting me know." She took Savannah from Kiana and sat in a nearby rocking chair. "You look like you've had a rough day."

Kiana bit back a laugh. "*Rough* wouldn't be the word I'd use to describe it."

At least she'd taken the time to glance in a mirror on the way over and make sure she didn't have lipstick or mascara smeared all over her face.

"Care to talk about it?" Denise cradled Savannah in her arms and rocked back and forth like she had all the time in the world.

"The gala sold out." Start with the simple stuff before delving into the dilemma that was Frank Kelly.

"That doesn't sound like a bad thing to me."

"It's not, but we'd actually sold more tickets than we'd intended, so I've been rushing around all day trying to make sure we had enough room and food for everyone."

Denise nodded, her gaze flickering over Kiana's dress. "But I take it you weren't putting in late hours at the office dressed like that."

Well, technically she still was in her office when Madison called. She'd just been riding her post-orgasmic high after riding Frank.

Kiana's skin warmed at the memory of his big hands on her bare skin. They had been so soft, gentle, adoring. So unexpected from a man of his size and reputation.

Denise cleared her throat and jerked Kiana from her reverie. "I gather from that dreamy look on your face that the day wasn't as rough as it seemed."

Kiana replied with an embarrassed laugh. "No, it wasn't. I had another date with Frank."

"He sounds like a nice young man."

A month ago, she would've laughed at the idea of Frank being a "nice young man." She only knew him by his reputation both on and off the field. But now that she'd gotten to know him, she couldn't agree more with her stepmother's assessment. "He is. Especially considering our date got off to a rocky start."

"How so?" Denise glanced down at the toddler who was dozing quietly in her arms.

"I was so busy at work that I was almost an hour late. He actually showed up at my office to find out why I'd stood him up." Gooseflesh prickled her skin when she remembered her terror on his arrival. "I thought he'd react like Malcolm did when I'd done something wrong, and I freaked out a little."

Denise halted the sway of the rocking chair and stiffened. "He didn't hit you, did he?"

Kiana shook her head. "He didn't even raise his voice. That's what made my reaction so pitiful." She rubbed her arms. "I instantly expected the worst from him, and bless his heart, he'd done nothing wrong. He even came up with a workaround for our date."

"Which was?"

"Pizza and movie in my office." *Followed by hot sex for dessert.*

"Sounds like you need to latch on to him while you can." Denise rose and carried the sleeping toddler in her arms to the crib.

Kiana stiffened. "What is that supposed to mean?"

"It means it's time to start trusting people again instead of pushing them away. Not all men are like Malcolm."

"I sometimes find that hard to believe after seeing the string of losers my mother used to bring home."

"Your mother learned the hard way. And you learned from her mistakes. You were strong enough to get out of that bad relationship before you ended up like her, and now, your daughter is safe and spared from experiencing all the things you went through." Denise crossed the room and patted Kiana on the cheek. "I'm not worried about you, honey. You'll make the right decision. Just listen to your heart and your gut like I've taught you."

"I'm trying, Mama. It's just..." She glanced over at her sleeping daughter. "I'm scared."

"Nobody ever said love was easy, but you need to trust the person you're giving your heart to."

Denise's advice created a sharp pang in the center of Kiana's chest. Her stepmother had given her heart to her father, and he'd cheated on her. Yet, she'd somehow forgiven him.

Kiana continued to watch Savannah, silently counting her daughter's quick breaths while she mulled over her future with Frank. She might be able to trust him with her heart. But her daughter?

"Mama, do you think what Tre said is true? That Frank would run away if I told him about Savannah?"

"You know him better than me. What do you think?"

For all his playboy reputation, he'd shown her time and time again that he wanted her. His persistence hadn't waned. And the sex was beyond great. But was he father material?

Kiana wrapped her arms around her stomach, hoping it would squash the doubt radiating from her gut. "I think I need to tell him before I lose my heart."

"Sounds like a good plan. You don't have to introduce him to her right now, but he needs to know that you have priorities other than him."

"And if he decides not to continue our relationship…" She'd be upset. Maybe even a little crushed. But she'd move on. Her daughter was the most important thing in her life, and if someone wanted her, they'd have to want Savannah, too. "Well, I'm better off without him."

Denise hugged her. "See? You're strong enough to do what's right. You always have. Tre, on the other hand, is giving me gray hairs."

"What's that boy done now?"

"He left for Vegas this morning."

"Again? Didn't he just get back?"

Denise nodded and sank into the rocking chair again. "He claims he did so well there last week that he wanted to go back before his luck ran out."

"It's going to run out eventually." Kiana rubbed her temples and offered a silent prayer her brother wouldn't end up without a dime to his name again.

"That's what I keep telling him, but he won't listen to me. It's times like this that I wish your daddy was still alive. Marshall could always talk sense into that boy."

"Maybe he'll listen to Frank."

Denise chuckled as she rocked away. "If you think there's a chance it might work, then have at it."

A barking cough interrupted their conversation, and

Kiana rushed to the crib. Savannah's wheezes filled her ears when she picked up her daughter. "I think we need another breathing treatment."

"I'll tell the nurse."

Denise left the room to find some help while Kiana clung to her baby girl. She'd worry about Frank and Tre and everything else later. Right now, there was only one person who mattered. Savannah needed her. Everything else would have to wait until her daughter was breathing easier again.

And when things calmed down, she'd tell Frank about Savannah and see what happened.

Chapter Twelve

Frank threw his gym bag into the trunk and ran his fingers through his still-damp hair. All weekend, he'd punished his body with workouts from hell just to keep his mind off of Kiana. He physically craved her. But the dazed and confused feeling from Friday trumped his desire. She'd said she'd call, and she hadn't. She'd just fucked him and ran, leaving him with only a vague promise for later.

Okay, God, I'm getting the cruel irony here.

He slid into the car but didn't start the engine right away. He needed to know where he was going first. He pulled out his phone and called his brother. "Help me through this, Adam."

He recounted Kiana's odd behavior with the phone call and the fact that she hadn't contacted him. "I'm at the point where I need her to be honest with me, but I'm scared if I press her for answers, she'll push me away."

"Has Cully contacted you yet?"

Frank curled his fingers into his palm. "What does

Cully have to do with this?"

"He's been in Atlanta all weekend. Said he ran into some roadblocks that he needed to address in person. Something about sealed documents."

Shit! Cully had found something on her, just as he'd feared. But that was nothing compared to the sick feeling swirling in his stomach. "Why did you hire him?"

"Because you're not known for sound judgment when it comes to women, and the fact that *you* were suspicious made *me* suspicious."

"It's a little extreme, though, don't you think?"

"I'm just looking out for you. Besides, it seems you were right about her hiding something if Cully unearthed stuff on her."

"Any idea what?"

"Sorry, but Cully won't divulge anything until he has all the facts."

A private investigator with ethics. Great.

Frank started up his car. If he wanted answers now, then there was only one place to go. "Well, when you hear back from him, let me know if there's anything I should be aware of."

Sherita was typing away when he came to the foundation's headquarters, but she stopped when she spotted him. "Hello, Mr. Kelly."

"Mr. Kelly is my dad. Or my eldest brother. I'm just Frank." He pointed to the closed door in front of him. "Is she in?"

"Not right now." Sherita pushed back from her desk, her lips pursed as though she was deciding how much information to give up. "But she should be back within the hour."

"Good. I'll wait." He opened the office door and closed it behind him.

Nothing had changed since he'd left Friday night. The scent of her perfume still lingered in the air, accented only by the faintest tinge of sex. He glanced at the sofa, and his dick started to throb. Yeah, it had been good. Too good. And once wouldn't be enough.

He sat on the sofa, his legs stretched out in front of him, and closed his eyes. The memories from Friday night overwhelmed him to the point where he worried he'd grab Kiana for an instant replay the moment she walked in.

Damn it!

He jumped up from the sofa and walked around her desk. If he wanted answers, this would've been the perfect opportunity to go through her drawers and her computer. But his conscience cautioned him not to go there, to respect her privacy. There were some lines that didn't need to be crossed, and Adam had already crossed one for him by hiring Cully.

However, he couldn't ignore the picture of a baby in a frilly pink dress perched on her desk.

Cold sweat prickled the back of his neck as he stared at it. The baby had dark skin and a head full of curly black hair, but her eyes were just like Kiana's—big and framed by thick lashes.

The sound of women's voices trickled in from the outer office, and he backed away from her desk. He'd process what he'd found later. That is, if Kiana didn't answer his questions before then. He had just enough time to dive for the couch and strike a casual pose before the door opened.

Kiana strode in and went straight for her desk without looking in his direction.

Frank grinned. Sherita definitely played the part of the meddling assistant well. "Hello, Kiana."

She jumped with a squeak and turned toward him, her hand over her heart. "What are you doing here?"

Sherita poked her head in. "Oh, yeah, I forgot to tell you he was waiting for you. Toodles." She waved at them and shut the door.

Kiana dumped her briefcase in her desk chair, her eyes never leaving him. "You didn't answer my question."

"And you never called." He stood and tucked his hands into his pockets while he meandered toward her. "If I didn't know any better, I'd say you were trying to blow me off."

Her shoulders slumped as she sighed. "It's not like that."

"Then enlighten me. After all, what's a guy to think when a girl screws him senseless and then runs away?"

Her gaze flickered to the sofa, and she caught her bottom lip between her teeth. Desire flashed across her face. "Frank, I..." She paused and lowered her gaze to the floor. "We need to talk."

"No shit. Why do you think I'm here? It's not just because I want seconds."

Her head snapped up, her eyes wide.

Frank rested his palms on her desk. "And don't get me wrong. I *do* want seconds. I want them badly. But not before I get to the bottom of things."

That same lust-filled expression she'd worn seconds

before she jumped his bones flickered across her face, but unlike Friday night, she managed to hold back, much to his disappointment. "Fine, let's go for a walk."

"Can't we talk here?"

She peered around him at the sofa again. "No."

At least I know she wants me as much as I want her. He stepped back and gestured toward the door. "Ladies first."

***

I can do this. I can do this.

Kiana kept repeating the same phrase over and over again as she rode down the elevator with Frank. But every time she opened her mouth to tell him about Savannah, nothing came out.

Part of her wanted to have this conversation in private so that if Frank freaked out, it wouldn't become a public spectacle. But at the same time, she couldn't stay in that office. Not with him looking at her in a way that set her hormones into overdrive. She'd probably end up screwing him all over again, and she couldn't afford to do that right now. Not with a news crew set to arrive in an hour to make up for the interview she'd had to cancel on Saturday.

And not when her heart was jumping around in her chest with uncertainty.

They arrived at the ground floor. "Where to?" Frank asked.

"Do you mind going to Piedmont Park? It's just a few blocks away."

"Let's drive." He pointed to her high-heeled shoes. "I don't want to risk you tripping in those."

An irrational rumble of fear rolled through her stomach. Her head told her she could trust Frank, but her gut wasn't on board. "Fine, but I'll drive."

Traffic was relatively light for Midtown, and parking was easy to find. Within a few minutes, they were surrounded by the open, green space framed by the nearby skyscrapers. The breeze still carried a slight chill from the cold front that had come through on Friday, but the late March sun and her sturdy blazer were more than enough to keep her warm as they walked.

"What happened Friday night?" Frank asked, his hands rooted in his pockets.

Before or after we had sex?

Her breath shook as she blew it out. He'd opened the door, and it was up to her to take advantage of it. "I had a family emergency."

He skidded to a stop. "Your mom? Tre?"

She shook her head and prayed for courage. "No, my daughter."

For a moment, he stood there with his mouth hanging open, the perfect statue of a man in shock. It was just as she'd expected, right down to the panic in his eyes.

She silently cursed and started to turn away, but he caught her and pulled her back. "What happened?"

Not "Oh my God, you have a daughter."

Not "Holy shit! You have a kid?"

Not "Get away from me before you infect with me with kid cooties."

What happened?

And the warm glow in her heart overwhelmed the trepidation in her gut. "Savannah has asthma, and the weather change set her off. We just got her home from the hospital this morning."

Frank cursed and slid his hand along the side of his face like he'd just woken up. Seconds ticked by as he appeared to take it all in. "But she's going to be okay?"

"Yeah, for now." Kiana crossed her arms across her chest and resumed walking.

He caught up to her in three easy strides. "Why didn't you just tell me that on Friday?"

"Because I don't want too many people to know about her."

"Why?"

She'd already dropped one bomb on him, and he hadn't run away. Time for the second one. "She's Malcolm's kid."

His face lit up with understanding.

"I was six months pregnant when I finally got the nerve to get out of that relationship," she continued, her slow amble matching the pace of her confession. "There are restraining orders in place, but we both saw how well he adheres to them. I never want him to lay a finger on her. If it weren't for the foundation and my family, I would've left Atlanta a long time ago. But it's why I don't let too many people know where I live and why I don't let just anyone watch her when I go out."

He nodded but didn't say anything more. Several minutes passed in silence, but he remained at her side with his hands in his pockets. "So, what's next?" he asked at last.

"What do you mean?"

"What's next for us?"

Now it was her turn to skid to a stop. "Am I hearing you correctly?"

He arched one brow. "Depends on what you're hearing."

"You just found out that I have a kid, and you still want to go out with me?"

"I was asking you that." He closed the space between them. "The ball's in your court, Kiana. It always has been."

Her pulse quickened, but not from fear. She breathed in his scent and found peace. "You won't be offended if I don't introduce her to you for a while?"

He gave her a crooked grin. "I'm okay with easing into that part of the relationship, so long as you don't hold back on anything else."

"Meaning?" She leaned forward, waiting to see if he'd stumble back.

He wrapped his arms around her instead. "Any more secrets?"

There were some demons in her past, but nothing that would interfere with their relationship now. When the time came, she'd tell him about her hellish childhood. But for now, she'd revealed the biggest barriers to their relationship. "I think you know the important ones."

"Then I can live with that." He lowered his lips to hers in a soft kiss. "Let's get you back to the office for your interview. After all, I just spent a week in Florida missing you in order to bring in some more items for your fundraiser, and I don't want you to miss out on any free promo you can get for it."

"You know, you never told me exactly what you did down there." She looped her arm through his and started retracing their path. "Care to enlighten me on the way back?"

"If you'd looked on the auction site, you would've seen some of the stuff I got, but since you're giving me an opportunity to brag, let me *enlighten* you on how much you owe me."

She laughed at first, but when he started rattling off all the autographed items he'd gotten from dozens of players from multiple teams, her chest tightened. "Sweet Jesus, Frank, you're joking, right?"

"Nope. And if I had more time, I'd go to Arizona and pester those guys. Like I told you from the beginning, when I commit to something, I give it my all."

And judging by the way he was looking her, he would be just as earnest in his efforts to capture her heart.

She smiled up at him and squeezed his arm, glad she'd listened to her heart instead of her gut. She didn't know what the future held with him, but she looked forward to finding out. "Thank you, Frank. For everything."

***

Frank's thoughts remained uncharacteristically somber as he drove home from Kiana's office. She had a kid. A pretty little girl, if he was correct in assuming the picture he'd found on her desk was of her daughter. And it was that asshole's child.

He curled his fingers around the steering wheel and gnashed his teeth. What kind of man would hit his pregnant girlfriend? A stream of vicious thoughts ran through his mind. He didn't carry an ounce of regret for breaking Malcolm's jaw. He didn't even want to imagine what would've happened to that innocent kid if Kiana hadn't been brave enough to get away.

And that was what sobered him in an instant. Kiana had been strong enough to get out. Strong enough to put restraining orders in place and protect her child. Strong enough to hide her from him until she felt safe enough to share her secret, even if it meant jeopardizing her relationship with him.

He pulled into his driveway and was blindsided by how his big backyard would be perfect for a swing set. Sweat prickled his forehead. His stomach churned. *Shit, I'm not ready for all this.*

And yet it didn't stop him from imagining what it would be like to come home to something other than an empty house. To hear a childish voice squeal with excitement the moment he opened the door. To be tackled by half a dozen little bodies as soon as he set his stuff down, just like the way he and his brothers had greeted their dad when he'd come home from work.

Suddenly, the idea of an instant family didn't seem so terrifying.

He got out of the car with every intention of pouring a stiff drink as soon as he walked through the door. Anything to soothe his rattled nerves. And there was a full bottle of scotch in the liquor cabinet that was calling to him.

"Nice place you have here," a man said as Frank came into the kitchen.

Frank jumped, fear hammering through his veins. He tensed and curled his hands into fists while he searched for the nearest weapon. His defenses only went down a hair as Theodore Cully rose from the sofa and approached him with a smirk.

"But you really need to think about upping your security," the private investigator said with a dry sense of humor. "Way too easy to break in and help myself to your bottle of Macallan."

He shook his glass. There were only a couple of ice cubes left in it.

"As long as there's some left for me." Frank found the open bottle on the counter and poured himself a healthy dose on the rocks. "Is there a reason why you're here? I mean, besides proving that you could be a first-rate thief if you decided to go that route?"

Cully chuckled and set his glass down. "Just here to deliver the goods your brother requested."

He retreated to the sofa, giving Frank enough time to study the private investigator. Cully appeared to be in his late thirties or early forties judging from the gray at his temples, but his body was as lean and toned as an elite triathlete's. Frank had no idea what he'd done before coming to work for Kelly Properties. Adam and his father had both hinted that Cully had lived a colorful life before settling into the somewhat tamer profession of digging up dirt on people, and Frank wouldn't be surprised if breaking and entering was on the man's CV.

Cully handed him a plain manila envelope. "You were right to be suspicious about this one. Sealed court records and everything."

Frank eyed the envelope, unsure if he wanted to know its contents. Kiana had already shared with him the reasons why she didn't want anyone to know where she lived and why she couldn't go out with him on a moment's notice. She'd said she'd already revealed the important stuff. And yet, judging by the thickness of the envelope, there was plenty she hadn't told him about. He held the glass in his hand, wondering if the wetness along his palm was due to condensation or his own sweat. "Care to give me the highlights?"

Cully shook his head. "Not what I'm paid to do. But I will say Ms. Dyer is a very interesting woman. A little paranoid, but for good reason."

Frank already knew that. But the unknown terrified him even more. He liked Kiana. He trusted her. Hell, he could even be falling in love with her based on the fact he didn't feel the urge to run away scared shitless when she told him she had a kid. But would learning all her secrets ruin the good thing they had?

The private investigator placed the envelope on the counter and retrieved his things. He took a moment to scribble something on a pad of paper and tore off the sheet. "By the way, this is a much better security system. Your current one took me less than a minute to hack."

"Noted." Frank took the paper and followed it up by draining his glass of single malt scotch. The whisky burned all the way down to his gut but did little to ease the tension squeezing his chest. "Anything else?"

"Nope." Cully offered him a mock salute. "Always good doing business with your family. I'll see myself out."

Once he was alone, Frank stared at the sealed envelope for what felt like an eternity, still clutching the empty glass in his fist. He finally set it down before he shattered the thin crystal and picked up the envelope. It weighed more than he'd expected, and new knots formed between his shoulders. He held the equivalent of Pandora's box, and he waffled on whether he wanted to unleash the chaos ·it contained.

The image of her curled up on the sofa in fear last Friday replayed through his mind, and a bitter taste filled his mouth.

But if I want a future with her, I need to know her past, if only to avoid terrifying her like that again.

After another glass of whisky, he worked up the courage to break the confidential sticker holding the flap down and slid out the papers inside.

The first thing that greeted him was a picture of a woman with blond hair and blue eyes. Cully had paper-clipped it on top of a stack of papers labeled as "Mother."

Frank studied it for moment. The woman was young and pretty in a late-1980s sort of way. Kiana had inherited her mother's full lips and high cheekbones, but when he pulled the photo aside, the next thing he saw was an arrest record.

Shannon Marie Tisdale, age 22. Extortion.

Frank silently cursed and turned the page.

Shannon Marie Tisdale, age 23. Fraud.

The few pages contained more arrest records ranging from petty theft to possession to prostitution. Just when he began to wonder if they'd locked up Kiana's mother and thrown away the key, he landed on a photocopy of a newspaper article.

"Forsythe County Woman Found Slain in Home."

His blood ran cold, but he kept reading.

> *Shannon Tisdale, age 30, was found dead of multiple gunshot wounds in her home at approximately 11:21 PM last night. Police had been called to the victim's*

home by her eight-year-old daughter to break up a domestic dispute, but the victim was already deceased when they arrived. 911 records are not available at this time, but a detective at the scene confirmed that the victim had been alive when the call was made and that the victim's boyfriend, Duane Filbert, has been taken into custody. Mr. Filbert had been arrested earlier this month for domestic assault against the victim and was out on $5,000 bail.

Frank reread the article half a dozen times, growing more and more nauseated each time he came to the part about the call being placed by the woman's eight-year-old daughter. *Jesus.* Kiana had been there the night her mother was murdered. She'd been the one to call for help. And the police had arrived too late to save her mom.

He poured another glass of the scotch and took a sip before even contemplating the rest of the documents. He'd already learned more than he wanted to know. Kiana had plenty of demons in her past, all right, but the fact she'd managed to get her shit together and move past them made her even more precious to him. Now he understood her protective stance when it came to both her daughter and her personal life, and he would wait for her to tell him more about her past when she was ready.

He gathered up the rest of the documents and ran them through the shredder. He'd seen enough. A minute later, they were nothing more than a wastebasket full of bits of paper.

The sheet of paper Cully had given him with the name of the better security system caught his attention. He carried it over to his computer and entered the name to find a local retailer. If he could ever convince Kiana to stay the night at his place, he wanted her to be as safe as possible, starting with a top-of-the-line security system.

Chapter Thirteen

Kiana tugged up the bodice of her strapless yellow chiffon dress and prayed she wouldn't suffer a wardrobe malfunction before the evening was over. The dress had fit perfectly at the shop when she'd tried it on last month, but the stress of setting up the fundraising gala had shed ten pounds from her frame, most of it coming from her bust. Too bad it hadn't come off her booty. That was one area where she had more than enough to spare.

Sherita motioned for her to join her in the corner of the ballroom and handed her two silicone pads. "Slip these into your bra."

"I never thought I'd be going back to stuffing my bra," Kiana muttered as she tucked the pads under her breasts. A few jiggles later, her cleavage filled out the sweetheart neckline to where she no longer feared that the gown would slip low enough to expose a nipple. "Thanks."

"What are best friends for?" Sherita waved her arm out at the empty but fully decorated ballroom. "Ready for this?"

"Ready as I'll ever be." She patted her hair one more time to make sure no more curls had slipped free from the tangle of bobby pins holding them back in the updo she'd gotten earlier this afternoon. "What are our numbers so far?"

Sherita pulled out her iPad and tapped on the screen. "The gala is sold out at eight hundred attendees. The items here for the silent auction are estimated to be worth two hundred and twenty thousand dollars, and the online auctions are currently estimated to bring in another six hundred and ninety thousand dollars."

Kiana's eyes widened as she added up the numbers. "Holy cow, Sherita, we may crack a million dollars."

"If we do, you need to give Mr. Well Connected a very special thank-you gift." She nodded toward the man with bright red hair coming their way. "And I hope it includes some kinky stuff."

Kiana's cheeks flamed. She elbowed her friend, but she couldn't take her eyes off Frank. The cut of his tux framed his broad shoulders and added an air of refinement to his muscular physique. His hair burned like fire under the dim light of the ballroom's chandeliers, but it paled in comparison to the heat radiating from his pale blue eyes.

His grin widened as he joined them. "You ladies look lovely this evening," he said even though his gaze never strayed from Kiana.

"You look very nice, too."

"Of course I do. Just because I'm a dumb jock doesn't mean I can't pull off the James Bond look from time to time." He smoothed down the satin lapels of his jacket and straightened his bow tie. "But I'll look even better with a lovely lady like yourself at my side."

He offered her his arm, and Kiana took it with a roll of her eyes. "Do you ever stop?"

"Is there a reason why I should?" He lowered his mouth to her ear. "You look as delicious as lemon meringue pie. Sweet, but tempting me to taste you."

He pressed his lips to the sensitive area behind her earlobe, and a flash of desire shot straight to her core, making her knees wobble. She hadn't had any more dates with him since she'd told him about Savannah—mostly because she'd been so focused on making sure the gala went off without a hitch—but that didn't stop Frank from snagging a few passionate kisses whenever he could.

Of course, with the front doors to the ballroom about to open, this wasn't the time or place to screw him senseless like she wanted to. "Behave," she said through a clenched smile. "Tre is staring at us."

"Let him. For all he knows, we're going over last-minute preparations for the evening." He trailed his fingers along her bare back. "For example, I'm dying to know if you're wearing those sexy granny panties with the secret opening tonight."

Dear Lord, if he didn't stop, she'd make a spectacle of herself by dragging him to whatever private location she could find just to ease the ache building between her legs. As it was, her skin was growing so warm, she was in danger of breaking out in a sweat and ruining her makeup. "Not tonight."

"Too bad. I really enjoyed them. Almost as much as I enjoyed you."

There was just enough innuendo in his voice to raise a

whimper into her throat. "Frank Kelly, if you don't behave…"

He laughed and added a few inches of much-needed space between them. "You're so sexy when you're flushed."

"Maybe so, but this is supposed to be an upscale event, so please practice some decorum."

"Yes, ma'am. I promise to be a perfect gentleman." But the wicked glint in his eye told her he'd only stay that way until she told him to stop.

She guided him to where Denise and Tre stood ready to greet the attendees.

Her stepmother squeezed her hand. "You've done such a beautiful job, Kiana. Your daddy would be proud."

"It'll only be a success if we raise the money we need to carry out his mission." She nodded to the ballroom staff waiting by the door. "It's six thirty, so let's get this party started."

The next hour passed in a blur. As soon as the doors opened, the attendees started pouring in. Atlanta's elite had turned out in full force, and she could only pray they brought their checkbooks with them. Soft music played in the background while Miss Rosa's staff wandered the room with polished trays carrying mouth-watering delicacies. Hundreds of voices created a low hum that drowned the pounding of her heart, and heat from the crowd chased away the early April evening chill that had earlier filled the empty ballroom.

Kiana worked her way around the room with Frank firmly at her side. He introduced her to some of the guests he'd invited, starting with some of his teammates and working his way up to local celebrities. She smiled until her cheeks ached and chatted until her throat felt raw, but inside, she could barely suppress her excitement. The evening was turning into everything she'd hoped it would be.

She was just about to beg Frank to take her to the table so she could rest her feet when she turned around and came face to face with Doug Boutry. Her mouth went dry, and all the small talk she'd so easily made all evening failed her.

Frank gave his friend a fist bump. "Dougie, you made it."

"Of course I did, bro. I gotta make sure my autographed jersey goes for at least a grand." The basketball star turned his attention to her. "Frank's been talking nonstop about you and your foundation, and I want to do what I can to help."

She opened her mouth, but no words came out, and she found herself nodding like an idiot.

"Give her a minute, Dougie." Frank grinned and winked at her. "She's a huge fan, but if she saw the sorry-ass way you played *Assassin's Creed*—"

"Don't be dissin' my Xbox skills in front of a hot woman, Kelly." Doug straightened so he had a couple of inches of height over Frank and glared down at him. "If I didn't know better, I'd say you were worried I'd steal her away from you."

"Hah!" Frank tried to act cocky, but a brief flash of worry flickered across his face when he looked at her.

It was no contest. Kiana looped her arm through Frank's. "Sorry, Dougie, but I'm already spoken for."

"Well, if you change your mind…" Now it was Doug's turn to wink at her before chasing after someone he knew.

"You know you can talk to him," Frank teased. "It's just Dougie."

"I know, but I have all the man I need tonight." She smiled up at Frank and wondered how he'd managed to carve out a place in her heart so quickly. "Care to dance?"

His grin slipped. "Dance?"

"Yes, dance. I thought you had plenty of moves." She led him to the small dance floor where couples swayed to the gentle jazz melody. "Besides, this is white people dancing. It should be easy for you."

But when she wrapped her arms around his neck, a look of panic tightened his face. "Confession time."

"What?"

"I have no problem gettin' down in a club, but I haven't danced like this since junior high."

She guided his arms around her waist as though they were a couple at an awkward school dance. "And why is that?"

"Because if I make an ass of myself at a club, I can blame it on a number of things. Too much booze, for example. But this…" His voice trailed off, and he stared at her face. "When I'm dancing this close to you, I forget about everything else around me."

"Then keep your eyes on me and know I'm right here with you until the end."

"Even if I step on your feet?"

She laughed as she pressed her forehead to his. There was little danger of that. For all his hesitation, Frank glided across the floor with the same ease he'd demonstrated

155

when they danced the salsa weeks ago. In his arms, she felt safe, secure, loved. And it was all too easy to fall in love with him on the dance floor.

***

The ballroom had six bars set up around the perimeter, but Frank zeroed in on the one his friends and teammates had claimed for most of the evening. He ordered a scotch for himself and a glass of champagne for Kiana before asking Tre, "How are you doing?"

"Okay, I suppose. Bored with all the fancy nonsense."

A chill coursed down his spine, and Frank hesitated a moment before asking, "I meant, how are you doing overall?" When Tre didn't answer right away, he added, "I saw the notice."

"So?" Tre replied with a healthy dose of surly attitude.

Neither of them wanted to say out loud that Tre had been released from the team that morning.

"Have you told them?" Frank nodded to where Kiana and Denise were chatting at a table.

"Why? So I can distract them from all the wonderful work daddy's little girl has done?" Tre slammed his glass down on the bar and indicated that he wanted a refill. "Besides, my agent is already on it. Some other team will pick me up. Everything's going to be all right."

He sounded like he was trying more to convince himself instead of Frank, especially with the way his voice wobbled at the end.

"I hate to lose you as a teammate."

"More like you're worried that I'm going to run you over when I'm playing for someone else." He took his full glass and stumbled forward. "But keep it just between us for the night. I don't want Mama and Kiana worrying."

"Don't worry, Tre. I'm sure I can find plenty of ways to distract your sister."

Tre cut him off, his eyes turning into narrow slits. "What are you playing at with her?"

"I'm not playing at all. I like her, and I hope you're okay with us dating."

Tre's eyes narrowed even more, and his chest puffed out. "Watch it, Romeo. Kiana's been through enough shit already, and she doesn't need any more from you."

Shit was putting it mildly, based on what little he'd read from Cully's investigation. "I know. She told me about Malcolm and Savannah, and that's why I'm on my best behavior around her."

Tre fell back a step and blinked several times, his expression going lax with surprise. "She told you about Savannah?"

Frank nodded. "A couple weeks ago, actually. I haven't met her yet, but I understand why Kiana wants to shelter her."

"Fine." Tre took a long drink from his glass. "Just remember—I'm watching you. You're my friend, but she's my sister. Got it?"

"Noted."

Frank turned his attention back to the woman who'd held it from the moment he entered the ballroom. He meant what he'd said earlier about her being tempting enough to taste. The yellow dress she wore exposed a swath of silky skin along her back and shoulders that practically invited him to press his lips to it, and the soft pink of her lips was innocent and yet delectably kissable.

Of course, he wanted to do more than kiss her. Two weeks had passed since the "date" in her office, and he'd been suffering a string of nightly hard-ons from wanting to be buried inside her again. But with the gala so close, they'd had very little alone time. He only hoped that once this evening was over, he'd be able to enjoy more than just a few naughty kisses from her.

CHAPTER FOURTEEN

Kiana wasn't sure if her giddiness was due to the champagne she'd consumed throughout the evening, the warmth of Frank's hand pressed into the small of her back as he peered over her shoulder, or the final number on Sherita's iPad. "Is that correct?"

"I triple checked it just to make sure," her best friend replied. "The final tally for the evening's auction was $267,519."

Kiana sank back in a chair. The gala had ended less than an hour ago, but the ballroom's staff was still cleaning up around them. "That exceeded our expectations."

"That's because some people flat out gave us donations." Sherita pulled out the bank bag and showed her the contents. "Look at all the checks we collected."

Denise clapped her hands and then pinched Kiana's cheeks. "I knew if anyone could pull this off, it was you. Your daddy would be so proud."

Kiana's joy was tempered by the sulk forming on Tre's

face. She reached out to him and pulled him closer. "We all did it."

But she knew where the real thanks lay. Her smile widened when she looked up at Frank. "I couldn't have done this without all of you."

"Just come out and say it, Kiana. It was all due to my pretty face on your ad." Frank gave her his cheeky grin before bending down to place a chaste kiss on top of her head.

"Oh, yes, Frank, it was all you," she said, tongue in cheek.

It wasn't far from the truth, though. The amount of support he'd been able to gather from the sports community still boggled her mind. If her estimations were correct, he'd been responsible at least in some part for eighty percent of the money they'd raised.

"You've all done well." Denise covered her mouth as she yawned. "And if y'all will excuse me, it's time for this old lady to get to bed."

"I'll take you home, Mama. Just give me a minute." Tre rose from the chair he'd been slouching in for most of the evening and approached her. "If you want, I can deposit the checks in the morning for you."

"I can do it."

"Kiana, please, let me do something. Besides, you deserve a few days off after all the hard work you've put in."

She was too tired and too tipsy to argue, especially when her brother was finally making an effort to help with the foundation. She nodded to Sherita. "Let him take the bank bag."

Her friend zipped it up and secured it with a zip tie. "Here you go, ready to deposit. I even filled out the forms for you."

"Thanks." Tre's mouth twitched as he took the bank bag, and he lowered his gaze. "Mama's right, you know. You did a good job, Kiana."

"Thanks, Tre." It was the closest thing to a compliment she'd gotten from him since she'd taken over the foundation.

Her brother left the ballroom with Denise, and Sherita bounced up from her chair. "And now that I'm off the hook, I'm out of here, too. Have a wonderful weekend, you two."

Her best friend was all but basically telling her to hook up with Frank while she had a chance. Not that the thought hadn't crossed her mind more than once this evening. As good as Frank looked in his tux, she wanted to get him out of it. She just wished she could pay Madison to stay overnight with Savannah so she could enjoy a sleepover at Frank's house.

"Can I walk you to your car?" he asked, still playing the part of a complete gentleman all too well.

But now, she didn't want the gentleman. She wanted the bad boy.

She rose from the chair slowly, employing every seductive move she could. She held his gaze. She nibbled on her bottom lip. She pressed her hand over the place where his heart pounded, followed by the curves of her body. "I suppose you could."

His pulse jumped, and he licked his lips, but he made no move to touch her. "Or?"

"Or you can give me a ride home." The frantic pace of her heart matched his, but for an entirely different reason. She was taking a risk with him. She was going to reveal where she lived. But her gut offered no warnings. She trusted him. "After all, I did have several glasses of champagne, and my place isn't too far from here."

He swallowed hard and covered her hand with his.

His hesitation kicked her fear into overdrive. Maybe she'd misread him. Maybe he was done playing the boyfriend role now that the fundraiser was over. Maybe he was secretly freaked out over the fact that she had a kid. She lowered her eyes and started to turn away.

Frank pressed his other hand on her ass and kept her pressed against him. A rough edge laced his voice as he asked, "And then?"

"And then we'll see where the evening goes."

Her reply sounded too polite, too calm for what she really wanted. Inside, she was screaming that she wanted to drag him to bed and keep him there for a solid week. She wanted to rip his clothes off and admire the hard muscles of his body. She wanted to take his cock deep in her mouth and watch him writhe in pleasure as she made him come. And then, once he was hard again, she'd ride him like she had that night in her office until she came.

She didn't need to say all that, though. The hunger in his eyes told her he knew exactly what she had in mind. He grabbed her wrap and draped it over her shoulders. "Let's get you home."

She hadn't been lying when she said her place was nearby. Her Buckhead condo was a mere ten-minute drive at this time of night, which was perfect. Any longer, and she might have been tempted to lower her head to his lap while he drove. It was hard enough as it was to keep her hands off him.

Touching him, measuring his response to her touch, would have done wonders to ease her rattled nerves. She was venturing out into unfamiliar territory. For the first time since she'd had Savannah, she was inviting someone outside of her close circle of family and friends into her home. For the first time in almost two years, she was bringing a man home with her. She knew without a shadow of a doubt that Frank would never tell Malcolm where she lived. It was the other possible complications that worried her.

Frank stopped at the security gate that blocked access to the parking garage under her building and waited for her to give her code. Once she gave it and told him where to park, he eased his Maserati in the spot but didn't turn off the engine. He stared straight ahead. "Now what?"

"What do you mean?"

"I'm trying not to assume too much, Kiana. If you were any other woman, I'd assume an invitation back to your place meant only one thing. But you're not like other women, and I feel like I'm walking on eggshells all the damned time because as much as I want you, I don't want to scare you. I know what you've been through. I know you have a daughter to protect. And I don't want to sink to the level of that asshole by stepping over the line."

Her chest tightened to the point where it was hard to breathe. When she'd first met Frank, she'd been ready to believe he was nothing more than a player. But in the weeks that followed, she'd discovered a man worthy of her heart. And she trusted him with it, just like she trusted him with her secrets.

"Then let me cut to the chase. I want you to come upstairs with me. I want you to follow me to my bedroom. I want you to do all the things you said you'd do to me that afternoon in my office. But if you're not ready—"

He snapped his head in her direction. "I'm more than ready."

The wild desire in his eyes sent a shiver of delight coursing through her. "But we'd have to be quiet."

"I can be quiet." That cocky grin appeared. He turned off the engine and dashed around the car to open her door. When she got out, he pulled her into a searing kiss that heightened her own arousal. "I make no promises for you, though."

He was teasing her, but she had little doubt he'd make good on it.

She beckoned him to follow her through the security measures in her building. First was the key code and hand recognition pad to get into the building. Only a handful of people were registered on her list of people who could get past that point without registering with the guard in the lobby—Denise, Tre, Sherita, and Madison. Then there was the security guard in the lobby, followed by another key code for the elevator. And finally, when they got to her condo, a third key code unlocked the dead bolt of her steel door.

She'd chosen this building because she'd wanted to feel safe, but each layer of security added to her impatience. She couldn't wait to get Frank in her bed. But first, she had to play the part of a respectable matron until her nanny left.

Madison was reading a magazine when they opened the front door. Her eyes widened when she saw Frank, but she managed to keep her voice calm as she asked, "How was the gala?"

"An overwhelming success." Kiana removed her wrap and set her purse down on the small table in the foyer. "How was Savannah?"

"A perfect angel, as always." Madison gathered her things, her gaze flickering to Frank every few seconds. "Um, are you Frank Kelly?"

His grin widened. "The one and only."

Madison opened her mouth like she wanted to gush about what a huge fan she was, but the way his arms were wrapped possessively around Kiana's waist made it very clear they were an item. The nanny nodded once like she got the hint and dashed out of the condo. "See you on Monday."

Frank pressed his lips to Kiana's bare shoulder before whispering in her ear, "Now where is your bedroom?"

"This way. Just let me check on Savannah first. And remember—quiet."

"As a mouse." That didn't keep him from placing feather-light kisses along the nape of her neck as they went down the hall, his arms keeping her backside plastered against him until he took a detour into her room.

She wandered to the nursery and cracked open the door. Just as she'd expected, her daughter was sound asleep and oblivious to the world around her. Assured that everything was as it should be, she tiptoed back to her own room.

Frank pulled her back into his arms the moment she walked through the door. Once the door was closed, his kisses grew hungrier. His hands moved up to cup her breasts, and a low moan rumbled through his chest. The next thing she knew, her dress was puddled around her ankles, and she was left standing in a strapless bra and black lace panties.

"Although the granny panties had their merits, I like these, too." Frank ran his hands over her bare skin, caressing her curves as though she was a Victoria's Secret model instead of a mother with a little extra padding on her bones. "Of course, I'd like it even better if they were gone."

In a matter of seconds, he'd unhooked her bra and cupped her breasts in his greedy hands, his fingers pinching her nipples as his teeth grazed her shoulder. It was rough, but surprisingly sensual, and she allowed her body to relax against him.

"If I remember correctly, I said I was going to strip you naked and taste every inch of you." The raw want in his voice heightened her anticipation and made it all too easy to surrender to his control. He turned her around and backed her onto the edge of the bed, his eyes never leaving hers, his breaths coming sharp and quick.

She sat and tried to kick off her shoes, but he halted her. "No, allow me."

He removed the sling-back pump as though it were a glass slipper, trailing soft kisses her along her calf in the process. He did the same with the other sandal, going past her knee and up her thigh. When he came to her panties, she half expected him to rip them away in impatience, but he slid them down with the same gentle touch.

But that was where the gentleness ended. The next thing she knew, his mouth was firmly pressed between her legs, her thighs draped over his shoulders. He explored her sex with a series of greedy licks and nibbles, each flick of his tongue making her crave more.

She moaned and rolled her bottom to give him better access, but he clamped down on her hips and held her still while he drew her clit between his teeth. The shock of pain made her draw in a breath with a hiss, but the delightful rush that followed released the captive breath with another languid moan that belied the tension coiling deep inside. The less she tried to fight him, the better it felt. And when she surrendered completely to him, he took her over the edge.

She was still floating in bliss when he whispered her name. She opened her eyes a crack to find him staring down with a mixture of want and wonder.

"Are you ready for more?" he asked.

She nodded and sat up to help him out of his clothes. A half-dozen passionate kisses hampered the process, but as soon as he'd kicked away his boxer briefs, she pulled him on top of her. His solid, muscular body contrasted with her softness. His erect cock pressed against her thigh, so hard, so thick. She wrapped her hand around him and stroked his length while he deepened the kiss.

He broke away, gasping for air. "Condom?"

"In my nightstand."

He fumbled for it, knocking over the lamp and the baby monitor in the process before retrieving one of the foil-wrapped packets she'd stashed there a week ago. She winced at the sound of the crash, but when she didn't hear any crying from the next room, she relaxed and wrapped her arms around him.

Frank slipped the condom on and wasted no time. He entered with a single thrust and smiled. "You feel like heaven, Kiana."

"So do you." He filled her completely, stretching her inner walls to the point it was almost painful, but in a good way.

The sting eased as he began to move inside her with slow, smooth strokes. He wedged his arms under her shoulders and propped up his weight on elbows that pressed against her sides. His thumbs massaged tiny circles along her neck to the same tempo as his kisses. There was nothing rushed or frantic about his pace. This wasn't a quick Friday night fuck. It was relaxed and easy, like a Sunday morning lovemaking session.

She embraced the indulgence of it and allowed her unspoken emotions to tumble out through her kisses. She was easily falling in love with Frank Kelly, and when she was in his arms like this, she forgot about her fears and worries. She felt only love.

Her orgasm caught her by surprise. Usually, the increasing tightness in the pit of her stomach signaled she was on the brink of coming, but the waves of pleasure rolled through without their precursor. She cried out his name as loudly as she dared while her inner walls clenched around him. He answered by saying her name in the same hushed tones before giving her one final thrust and shuddering with a halt as he found his own release.

"Damn it, Kiana," he murmured before collapsing and

rolling to his side. He reached for her and pulled her against him. "I could die a happy man right now, as long as I have you lying next to me."

She snuggled up to him and nodded, relishing the safe comfort of his arms. "I couldn't agree more."

***

A chill washed over Kiana's bare skin, followed by a shift in the mattress underneath her. It roused her from the sound sleep she'd been enjoying in Frank's arms, but she didn't fully wake until she heard Savannah crying. She bolted up in time to see the outline of a man leaving her room.

Panic tightened her throat. She grabbed her robe and slipped it on as she chased after him. Somewhere in the back of her mind, she knew it was just Frank, and that he would never hurt Savannah, but that did little to ease the fear in her gut.

She ran into the room and halted just as he was lifting the fussy toddler from her crib.

Savannah grew silent and stared up at him with round eyes.

Frank had managed to pull his pants on before leaving the room, but that was all. He shifted her into the crook of his arm, cradling her like an oversized football against his bare skin. After a few awkward attempts to rock her, he finally settled on a rhythm that soothed her. "There," he murmured to Savannah. "That's better, right?"

Her daughter continued to watch him with her dark eyes.

"Okay, now let's see if I can make it to the rocking chair without making you cry." He turned around and halted when he saw Kiana standing in the doorway. A sheepish smile lifted the corners of his mouth. "Um, I…"

Savannah started to fuss again, and he went back to swaying her from side to side with a rush of shushing noises. The toddler grinned up at him and reached for his face, completely taken with the stranger holding her.

"I hope I'm not overstepping my bounds, but you were sleeping so soundly, and when I heard her crying…" He paused and looked down at Savannah. "She's just as pretty as you are, Kiana."

Her heart did another flip, and she fell even more deeply in love with him right then. "Let me take her off your hands."

"No, I have her." He went back to rocking the little girl, adding a little bounce to his step as he paced the room. "That is, unless you're uncomfortable with me holding her."

"No, I'm not." She'd thought she would be, but despite the anxious way he kept watching Savannah while he tried to soothe her, she trusted him with her daughter. "Did you check her diaper?"

His face turned a shade paler. "Diaper?"

Kiana fought back a laugh. Here was a man who pummeled quarterbacks for a living, yet the mere mention of *diaper* terrified him. She motioned for him to meet her at the changing table. "Usually when she wakes up in the middle of night, it's because she wants to be changed."

Frank set Savannah down and stood back while Kiana changed the wet diaper. But as soon as she buttoned up Savannah's pajamas, he took her back in his arms. "Go back to bed. I've got this."

Kiana raised one brow in disbelief. "Are you sure?"

"Absolutely." He gazed down at her daughter's face and elicited a smile from the toddler. "See, she can't resist my charm."

She would've argued it was the other way around based on the way he couldn't take his eyes off of Savannah. Kiana stood back as he carried the baby to the rocking chair and sat down. A minute later, he'd figured out how to hold her to his chest and was rubbing her back while he rocked.

The last of her fears faded. She'd been so worried that Frank would run away from her the minute she told him she had a daughter that she failed to see the gentle side of him. There was almost something comical, yet endearing about the way he shifted Savannah in his arms, taking extreme care not to upset her while appearing to be completely in over his head. But he didn't back away. He didn't run scared. He gave it his best effort, just like he claimed to do with everything else that was important to him.

He met her gaze and gave her a tight smile. "I've got this," he repeated.

Kiana returned to her bed and waited, inhaling the masculine scent of him that still clung to her warm sheets. Frank was already making his presence known in her home, and she liked it far more than she'd imagined she would.

Fifteen minutes later, he crawled under the covers beside her and pulled her into his arms. "Confession time."

"What?" she asked, her breath catching. Had he

171

changed his mind about continuing their relationship now that he'd met her daughter?

"I'm not going to lie. Little kids scare me shitless. I mean, they're so little and delicate, and I'm…not." He paused and drew in a deep breath. "But I think I can handle Savannah."

"You think?"

"Yeah," he said with a laugh. "I mean, that whole diaper thing might take me a while to figure out, but when I look at her, I see you, and that makes the effort worth it."

She looked up and found him smiling down at her. "It does?"

"Yeah." He brushed her hair back from her face and caressed her cheek. The tenderness in his gaze was only lightened by a hint of a mischievous glint. "I hope you don't mind sharing me with her."

"Not at all." She lowered his lips to hers and kissed him with all the love that was overflowing her heart. "You're something else, Frank Kelly."

"Haven't I been telling you that from the beginning?" he teased before kissing her again.

***

Frank awoke to an empty bed and a sense of bewilderment. It took several long seconds for him to recognize the strange room. Scenes of the night before flashed through his mind, from Kiana's commanding presence at the gala to the way she'd come in his arms. But it was the babble of a small kid that made his heart stutter for a few beats.

Ever since he'd found out about Kiana's kid, he'd

known he was in over his head. If he hadn't wanted her so badly, he might've toyed with the idea of running away. But she wasn't trying to make him an instant daddy, and he respected that. Actually, he was more relieved than anything else. It gave him time to come to terms with the fact that Kiana and Savannah were a package deal. He couldn't have one without the other.

But he still couldn't explain last night. He'd heard Savannah stirring over the baby monitor he'd knocked to the ground earlier that night, but Kiana had been sleeping so soundly, she didn't move when the first calls for *Mama* came in over the airwaves. He bounced back and forth with waking her, but in the end, he figured he could handle a kid. Or at least, peek in on her and make sure she was all right.

The moment Savannah looked up at him with those big brown eyes, he was lost.

The only time he'd been around a baby was the few peeks he'd gotten of Dan's fiancée's little preemie in the incubator. He'd known better than to attempt to touch a baby that tiny, especially since Camille had been born with some sort of condition where her guts were outside her stomach. But Savannah seemed sturdy enough for him to handle, and after a few awkward attempts, he figured out how to hold her and keep her happy.

He found his clothes and got dressed, realizing his tux was too overdressed for a Saturday morning. He kept it at just the shirt and pants and ventured out of the bedroom.

Kiana was making funny faces at her daughter, who resided in her highchair like a little princess on a throne. Savannah squealed in delight and clapped her hands before stuffing a handful of cereal into her chubby cheeks. They were so wrapped up in their little game that they didn't notice him until he tossed his jacket on the back of one of the tall chairs that lined the kitchen island.

A hint of color flooded Kiana's cheeks, making her look even more tempting than before. "Good morning, Frank."

"Morning." He sniffed the air, catching notes of sausage and cheese. "What smells so good?"

"I'm making a quiche. I usually make one on the weekend and eat it during the week." She glanced over her shoulder at the oven. "It should be ready in about ten minutes, if you'd like some."

He was hungry enough to eat the whole thing, but he'd try to restrain his appetite. "Sounds good."

Savannah offered him a handful of soggy cereal, and Kiana rushed in to take it. "Sorry about that, Frank."

"Why? She was just trying to hold me over until breakfast is ready." He sat on the chair closest to Savannah's high chair and poked her in the center of her tummy to tickle her. She rewarded him with a huge grin that eased his anxiety. "See? She likes me."

The soft glow of admiration coming from Kiana's eyes was all the reward he needed. "Yeah, she does."

"And can you blame her?" He continued to search for more ticklish spots, delighting in each giggle he elicited. "I just have a way with the ladies."

"No arguments from me." She came around the island and draped her arms around his shoulders. "You don't have to stay if you don't want to, but before you go, I just wanted to say thank you."

He reached for her hips by instinct, then slid back toward that delicious ass of hers. "Trying to get rid of me so quickly?"

"No, I'm not." The pink spots returned to the center of her cheeks. "What I was trying to say is that I don't expect you to feel comfortable with Savannah around right away, so if you're not, then there's no pressure, and you can leave whenever you feel like it."

"I know." He pulled her closer to him, looking up at her beautiful face. Even without her makeup, she was gorgeous. "But I like where I'm at right now."

She murmured his name just before her lips brushed against his in an innocent kiss.

He dug his fingers into her ass and held her against him, wanting more. She did that to him. Just when he worried he'd overstepped his bounds, she responded by deepening the kiss. He slipped under the hypnotic spell she wove with every sensuous flick of her tongue and forgot they were not alone.

The childish voice asking for "More" brought him crashing back down to reality.

Kiana gave him an apologetic smile and backed away. "Sorry about that."

"Don't be." He grabbed the cereal box from the island and poured some more into Savannah's bowl. "So, do you have any plans for today?"

"No, why?" The oven timer dinged, and Kiana retrieved the quiche from the oven.

His mouth watered from the scent. If it tasted half as good as it smelled, he'd be in heaven.

The prospect of breakfast distracted him, but he finally

remembered why he'd asked about her plans. "Have you taken Savannah to the aquarium yet?"

"I think she's a little young for that."

"Nonsense. Several of the guys on the team have taken their kids, and some of them are only a year old." He tickled Savannah's foot, his chest tightening with every giggle he won from her.

Kiana chewed her bottom lip and leaned on the counter. "I'll have to think about it."

"I'll come with you, if you want. No one's going to bother her if I'm around."

She laughed. "You're Frank Kelly. I'm going to have to hire a set of bodyguards to keep your fans at bay."

"I'm sure I can be discreet." He ran his hand through his trademark feature—his bright red hair. "Maybe a baseball cap will do the trick."

"Okay, fine. When would you like to go?"

"This morning too early for you?" He was already picturing how wide Savannah's eyes would get when she saw the whale sharks swim by.

"You're still wearing last night's tux."

"Easily taken care of." He pulled out his phone and called his personal shopper at Nordstrom in Phipps Plaza. Within a few minutes, he was assured that he'd have an outfit ready to pick up in half an hour. "I'll have new clothes waiting for me after breakfast."

Kiana placed a slice of quiche in front of him. "That easy, huh?"

"Yep." He dug into the savory egg pie studded with cheese, mushrooms, spinach, and sausage. A happy sigh rose from his gut. "This is as delicious as its maker."

Kiana swatted him with a dish towel, but he didn't miss the glow of pride radiating from her smile. She broke off a small slice and blew on it before offering it to Savannah. It was like a scene from one of those magazine ads or a commercial.

A perfect family sitting around the table, enjoying breakfast.

He'd never pictured himself as the sort of guy who'd be a family man, but the longer he sat in Kiana's kitchen, the more comfortable it felt. It was as though he belonged here. And if he had a chance, he'd make sure there would be many more mornings like this in their future.

CHAPTER FIFTEEN

Kiana waltzed into her office late Monday morning like a kid who'd just returned to school after spring break. Her weekend with Frank and Savannah couldn't have been more perfect. On Saturday, they went to the aquarium, where Frank had lifted her daughter onto his broad shoulders for most of the afternoon so she could have a better view of the fish. On Sunday, he invited them to his home in Roswell for lunch. Savannah appeared to be frightened by the vast grassy lawn, but after a few minutes, she was ordering Frank to pick the dandelions that grew along the perimeter for the bouquet she was making. And he indulged the toddler's every whim.

He also indulged Kiana's every whim, too, once Savannah was sleeping. The weekend had been filled with quick, hot sex during Savannah's naps and long, sensual lovemaking sessions into the wee hours of the morning. She'd lost count how many times she'd come, but every encounter left her eager for the next one.

Sherita gave her a knowing grin. "Looks like someone

had a fun weekend, judging by that glow in your cheeks."

Kiana dropped her briefcase down beside her desk and twirled around in her chair. "*Fun* doesn't even begin to describe it."

"And I suppose Mr. Hottie is responsible for it all?"

Kiana giggled as though they were back in junior high and she was spilling the details of her first kiss. "You could say that."

"I knew you two would hit it off." Her friend grabbed one of the chairs and pulled it up to the desk. "Care to share a few tidbits?"

She pressed her lips together, trying to decide how much she was willing to divulge. "He's good in bed."

"Tell me something I couldn't guess."

"And he's really good with Savannah."

Sherita sat up straighter, her mouth open. "Hold up a minute. You introduced him to your baby girl?"

Kiana nodded, a smile forming on her lips as she remembered how well he handled her daughter. "He's good with her."

"Now I know you're head over heels for that boy, because there's no way you'd let him near Savannah if you only felt lukewarm about him."

"What can I say? Romeo's swept both of us off our feet."

Sherita grew serious. "And he's good to you, right?"

The underlying concern in her friend's voice relayed the true meaning of her question. Kiana nodded and reached for Sherita's hand. "He's as gentle as he can be to both of us."

"Good, because after all the shit you went through with

Malcolm, you deserve someone like him." Sherita gave her hand a little squeeze and got up. "I've been waiting for you to come in and give me the all-clear to start sending out some checks. We have kids who need equipment, and now that we have the funds to do so, let's not keep them waiting."

Back to business. She'd taken a moment on Saturday afternoon to log into the foundation's bank account and confirmed that Tre had deposited the checks like he said he would. She was hoping they would've cleared by today so they could start fulfilling their mission. But when she logged onto the account this morning, the balance had read only three thousand dollars.

Kiana blinked several times to see if she was missing a couple of zeroes, but no matter how much she stared the screen, the number didn't change.

"Sherita," she called, her voice an octave higher than normal. "Come over here and take a look at this."

Her friend dashed to her side and peered at the screen, her brows drawn together. "Is there something wrong at the bank?"

"I have no idea. I know the money from the gala was deposited on Saturday." She clicked on the account for more information. Sure enough, there was a long list of checks that had been deposited two days ago.

But it was the two hundred and seventy five thousand dollar withdrawal this morning that captured her attention and made her want to vomit.

Sherita picked up the phone and shoved it into Kiana's hand. "Girl, I'd be calling them right now to find out what happened to your money."

It wasn't her money. It was the foundation's. It belonged to all those kids her father wanted to protect by giving them proper helmets and pads. It belonged to those who genuinely needed it, not her. And yet, when she got someone from the bank on the line, she said in a shaky voice, "This is Kiana Dyer of the Marshall Dyer Foundation, and there seems to be a problem with my account."

The person on the other line answered her questions. But as the information starting rolling in, her stomach was wracked with dry heaves.

Someone with access to the account had withdrawn the money.

And that meant either Denise or Tre.

***

Frank had just stepped out of the shower when his phone rang. The caller ID listed Kiana's name, and he picked it up, hoping to hear the sweet, sexy drawl in her voice as she suggested they meet up later this afternoon.

Instead, he heard a tight note of panic in her voice. "Frank, do you know where Tre is?"

"No, why?"

A muttered curse answered him, and the muscles along his neck tightened.

"Kiana, what's wrong?"

"I need to find Tre."

"Is something wrong? Your mom—?" He caught himself. Kiana hadn't shared her birth mother's past with him, and he wasn't quite sure if she thought of Mrs. Dyer as her mom.

"No, Denise is fine." A sharp inhalation filled the line,

and he pictured her biting her bottom lip the way she did when she was trying to make an important decision. "It has to do with the foundation."

"Can I do anything to help?"

"I—"

"Don't cut me out," he interrupted the moment he heard a note of hesitation in her voice. "I'm as committed to it as you are."

"I know, which makes this mess all the more complicated." She sighed. "Come to my office, and I'll fill you in. I don't want to talk about it over the phone."

"I'll be there as quickly as I can."

"And Frank, if you can get a hold of Tre, I'd appreciate it."

"Will do."

He hung up and got dressed in record time while calling Tre's cell three times. The third time, he left a message. "Tre, this is Frank. Kiana's worried about you. Give her a call when you get a chance."

There. Nothing too extreme, even though he wanted to throttle his friend for making Kiana worry like that. Just a message that would hopefully convince Tre to call his sister.

But when he arrived at Kiana's office, the furrowed lines on her face revealed that Tre still hadn't called. The dark circles smeared under her eyes told him she'd been crying hard enough to ruin her makeup, something he'd never seen her do. The confident, collected woman he'd known was gone, and in her place stood a frazzled woman near the breaking point.

She rushed into his arms. "Thank God you're here. I

don't know what to do."

"Start from the beginning, then." He placed a kiss on her forehead and led her to the sofa.

"Tre took the money."

He rubbed his ears, wondering he'd heard her correctly. "Tre did what?"

"The money from Friday night—it's gone."

His gut dropped like he'd just inhaled a dozen hot dogs in less than a minute. "But you checked the account on Saturday and said he'd deposited the checks."

"He did, but someone withdrew almost all the money from the foundation's account this morning. Only three people have access to that account. Me, Denise, and Tre."

Images of her birth mother's mugshots flew through his brain. Extortion. Fraud.

One glance at her distraught face, though, silenced any doubts before they could come to fruition. The Kiana he'd come to know wouldn't stoop to such measures. He'd witnessed her passion and dedication to the foundation enough to see she'd never be the one to steal from the children she wanted to help. It was the one thing that encouraged him to step up his game when it came to the fundraiser, and it was one of many things he'd come to love about her.

Love.

Holy shit. That word caught him off-guard. But as soon as he admitted to himself, his chest filled to the stretching point with the emotion. He'd fallen in love with her somewhere along the way, and it was just now hitting him like a linebacker blitzing a quarterback from the blindside.

"Have you spoken to Denise?"

She shook her head, and two tears streamed down her face. "I don't want to upset her."

"And are you certain Tre took the money?"

She nodded. "Ninety-nine percent sure. But why would my brother do such a thing? I know there's always been a bit of a rivalry between us, but this was our dad's dream."

Frank rubbed his thighs and stood. Suspicion snaked down his spine and mingled with the chill forming in his bones. Tre had asked him not to mention that he'd been cut from the team, but this was one secret that didn't deserve to be kept under wraps. "Tre was let go from the team on Friday."

Her lips parted, but no sound came out.

"He'd asked me not to say anything until after the gala, but if you're looking for a motive, you have one."

She winced like a person forced to accept the painful truth. "Be that as it may, we still need to find him."

"I left him a message to call you."

She gave a bitter laugh. "Great. It'll be mixed in with the dozen phone messages and texts I've sent him."

"Did you go by his place?"

"Sherita did. His car was missing."

He paced the room several times, still wiping his damp palms on his jeans. "Then you need to play hardball."

Kiana rose from the sofa and stopped him. "What are you talking about?"

"If the press gets hold of this, they'll have a field day dismantling the foundation, and they'll have no trouble pointing the finger at you based on your birth mom's history."

Her eyes widened, and she stumbled back. "How did you know—?"

"My brother hired a private investigator to check you out." He lowered his head, unable to bear the hurt and betrayal in her eyes, and tucked his hands into his pockets. "I told him none of that mattered to me, but he thought I should be careful before getting too involved."

Her jaw hardened, but she simply nodded.

"If it makes any difference, I stopped when I read the article—" He stopped and cursed under his breath. "Damn it, Kiana, I didn't need to read it all because none of it mattered to me. I know you, and I shredded the rest of the files without looking at them. But I thought you should know that."

She stood and stared out the window, her arms crossed over her chest and her back to him. "So what are you suggesting I do?"

"Call the cops."

CHAPTER SIXTEEN

Kiana's breath caught, amplifying the pounding of her heart through her overinflated chest. "He's my brother, Frank."

"I know, but you have to do something now before he runs, leaving you to clean up the mess." Frank closed the space between them and placed his hands on her shoulders. "I know it's a hard thing to do, and if it was one of my brothers, I'd feel the same way, but you have to hold him responsible for his actions."

"But if I turn him over to the police, he'll be arrested, and the foundation will still be hurt."

"Not if you can recover the money." Frank cupped her cheek and lifted her chin. "The longer you wait, Kiana, the worse it's going to look in the end. You can do this. And I'll be right here beside you until the end."

She wasn't sure if she should laugh or cry. He was throwing her words back at her. Only now, it was a far more serious situation than a simple twirl around the dance floor. And yet the determination in the set of his shoulders told her he wasn't going to abandon her. As angry as she'd been to learn some private investigator had been digging up all the sordid details of her past, the emotion had waned when Frank confessed to shredding the papers without reading them all. He didn't care about her past, and he was standing here beside her when trouble came knocking at her door.

She pulled his hand away from her face and nodded. "Then hold my hand as I do this." She added in a soft whisper, "Please."

He laced his fingers through hers and gave her a sympathetic smile.

Her fingers shook as she dialed the number for the police. Her voice didn't fare much better when she spoke to an officer, who said he'd contact the FBI with her information and get them involved.

By the time she hung up, she wanted to vomit. She was no better than Joseph's brothers in the Bible. She'd turned on her brother. She'd basically asked the cops to arrest him, just like she'd done to Malcolm. And she doubted Tre would ever forgive her.

The only thing that kept her grounded was the solid, firm hand wrapped around hers. Frank was still there with her. And when she was finished, he pulled her into his arms and held her close. "I can only imagine how hard that must've been for you, but you did the right thing."

"I hope you're right."

She had no idea how much time passed, but the sharp ring of her phone jerked her back to reality. She glanced at the screen, offering a silent prayer it was Tre, but saw Denise's number instead.

"What's this about Tre taking money from the foundation?" her stepmother asked as soon as she answered.

A slew of cuss words rolled through her mind, but she dared not utter them in front of Denise. "How did you hear about that?"

"It was on the news, along with a request to call the Georgia Bureau of Investigation if he's seen. I thought I'd dreamed it up, but someone from the FBI called me as it was airing."

Her stomach roiled, and she closed her eyes to keep the nausea from taking over. How had the media gotten wind of it? And worse, how big a hit would the foundation take because of Tre's actions? "I came into work this morning to find a significant chunk of the money from Friday night was missing from the account, and only the three of us have access to it."

"Lord Almighty, what has that boy done now?"

Kiana filled her in as best she could, adding in the fact he'd been cut from the team and was now unemployed. It gave him a motive, but why did he take so much? "At least there's one small silver lining to all this."

"And what's that?" Denise asked.

"The money from the online auctions still hasn't been deposited into our account, so we still have something to give to the kids."

"Oh, sweetie," Kiana's stepmother said. "I would come over there and give you a big hug, but I was told to wait here until some FBI agent arrived to question me."

"I'm so sorry about that, Mama. I know you wouldn't take a dime from the foundation."

"Don't apologize, dear. It's all part of the process." A faint chime sounded in the background. "Speaking of which, I believe the agents are here."

Kiana looked up to find a man and a woman in suits standing in the doorway of her office. "Same here. I'll let you know if I learn anything."

"Stay strong." Denise hung up, and Kiana faced the visitors.

The man held out a badge. "Special Agent Phillips, FBI. This is Agent Sculler from the GBI."

The woman held up a different badge with the state of Georgia embossed on it.

Kiana managed to stand, even though her knees wobbled under her. Thank God Frank was there to steady her. She extended her hand to them. "Kiana Dyer. Thank you for coming."

The afternoon passed in a blur as the agents questioned both her and Frank. They answered as truthfully as possible, but it didn't stop the agents from confiscating both her laptop and her work computer as evidence. At one point, Agent Sculler stepped out of the office to speak to Sherita. By the time the agents left, night had fallen, and the Atlanta skyline twinkled outside her window.

She rested her head on Frank's shoulder. "I've had to give testimony more times than I'd care to admit, but this was the hardest."

"How so?" he asked, pulling her into a hug.

"Before, I knew who the bad guy was, and I had no problem making sure he got what was coming to him. But my brother?" Her eyes stung, and her voice caught. "I think there must be a special level of hell reserved for people who betray their families."

"If there is, you don't belong there." Frank tipped her face up and ran his thumb along her bottom lip. "You've done nothing wrong."

"Then why do I feel so guilty?"

"Because you have a big heart that wants to see the good in everyone. Even fuckups like me."

"You are not a fuckup, Frank Kelly."

"Good, because I feel like one every damn day."

"I don't think Savannah sees you that way."

He placed his hand on her ass and pulled her against him. A playful smile crinkled the corners of his eyes. "That's nice, but I'm far more interested in what her sexy mama thinks."

"You already know what her mama thinks." But just to reassure him, she gave him a kiss that she hoped would ease any of his insecurities. She loved him. Loved him for helping out the foundation. Loved him for adoring her daughter. Loved him for being her rock today when most men would have hightailed it out of there once the shit hit the fan. And maybe she wasn't quite ready to say it in words, but she could definitely say it in her actions.

He ended the kiss as breathless as she was. "Keep that up, and we might end up on the sofa again."

The notion of a stress-reducing quickie tempted her, but as her pulse slowed, a heavy mantle of fatigue fell on her shoulders. "I'd love to, but I'm beat, and Savannah's waiting for me to get home."

"I understand." He placed a quick peck on her forehead and picked up her briefcase. "Why don't I give you a ride home?"

She nodded without even attempting to argue with him. She'd seen the news vans parked along the street, hoping to catch a glimpse of her. Thankfully, between the security guard downstairs and Sherita, none of them made it to her office.

The day had left her drained. All she wanted to do right now was curl up around her baby girl and hope the world would be a better place for her tomorrow.

Once they drove past the mob of reporters, the ride to her place was filled with silence. Frank seemed to understand why she wasn't in a talking mood, and he gave her some space. One question kept replaying through her mind as they drove through the streets of Atlanta.

Why?

Why did Tre do it? Was he that frightened about being let go from the team? Or was there some other reason why he did it? And if he gave her a good reason, would she be able to forgive him?

Frank entered the security code for her parking garage and parked in a visitor slot. "Want me to come up with you?"

She shook her head. "Thank you, Frank, but I just want to be alone right now."

"If you change your mind, I'm just a phone call away."

His hopeful grin tugged at her heart, and she squeezed his hand in return. "I know."

She climbed out of his car and made her way up to her condo with slow, heavy steps. She'd never been much of a drinker, but tonight definitely called for a glass of chardonnay. When she got to her place, she entered the key code, and the door flew open.

A hand grabbed her and yanked her inside.

The world spun in disorienting circles as she stumbled into the foyer. The door slammed shut behind her. Her heart jumped into her throat, only to come to a dead stop when the cold metal barrel of a gun pressed against her temple.

And from the other end of the gun, Tre glared at her, beads of sweat forming along his upper lip. The scent of alcohol hung on this breath, and but his words were anything but slurred. "We need to talk."

CHAPTER SEVENTEEN

Frank waited in the car until Kiana entered her building, but even then, he couldn't make himself pull away. She was trying so hard to be brave, to be strong, and all he wanted to do was cradle her in his arms until she fell asleep. Part of him hoped that she'd change her mind and call him when she got upstairs.

When ten minutes passed without a peep, he decided to cry uncle and started his engine. He circled the parking garage with agonizing slowness, wishing with every turn she'd call.

But it was the glimpse of a red Ferrari with the license plate that read "Wide Out" parked in Kiana's slot that formed ice in his veins.

Tre's car.

Frank threw his car in reverse and parked in the nearest open space, not giving a fuck if it was assigned to one of the building's residents. He ran to the door and tried entering Kiana's code, but his hand was too big to pass for hers.

Shit!

He was locked out of her building, and her brother was waiting up there to do God only knew what to her. If Tre had any clue the cops were after him, then his presence here wouldn't be a pleasant family visit.

The cops.

Frank pulled out the card Agent Phillips had given him and dialed the number.

"Special Agent Phillips," the man answered with the same dry, no-nonsense tone he'd used throughout the entire interrogation this afternoon.

"This is Frank Kelly. You're looking for Tre? Well, I've found him. He's at Kiana's."

"We'll be right there. Whatever you do, do not engage either of them. For all we know, she could've been hiding him there all day."

The suspicion in the agent's voice sickened him. Kiana would never be an accomplice to fraud. And yet, based on her birth mother's criminal history, he understood why the agent would think that was a possibility.

"Did you hear me, Kelly? Stay right where you are."

Like hell he'd stay down here when Kiana was in danger. "I'll try."

As he hung up, he heard the agent urging him to stay out of this, but it made no difference. He needed to know she was safe.

The next number he dialed was hers, and with each ring, he prayed she'd answer.

***

Kiana stood statue still, the only movement of her body coming from the frantic beat of her heart and the frequent glances around the room to look for Savannah. Flashbacks of the night her mother was murdered raced through her mind, each memory adding to the trembling in her hands. She never wanted her daughter to witness the things she had.

"Please, Tre," she whispered, her voice unsteady, "where's Savannah?"

"I told Madison to take her to the nursery and stay there until we were done."

Kiana breathed a small sigh of relief. Whatever Tre had in store for her, at least Savannah wouldn't have to see it. "Thank you."

He snapped his attention back to her, but thankfully lowered the gun. "Why did you do it?"

"I could ask you the same thing." She took care to keep her words calm and soothing without breaking eye contact with him. It was better than letting him know how terrified she really was.

He curled his lip and narrowed his eyes. "I was going to pay it back."

At least he wasn't denying that he took the money. With any luck, she might be able to discover the reason he felt the need to steal from their father's foundation. "I'm listening."

No judgment.

No questions.

Just a simple phrase to let him know that she cared to hear his side of the story.

It seemed to work. He wiped his hand over his face. "I was in trouble, Kiki," he started, using the nickname he'd given her when they were kids.

She kept her arms at her sides, scared that if she reached out to hug him like she wanted to do, he'd misinterpret it as an attack and shoot. "Why didn't you just tell me that?"

"Because..." He sucked in a breath and looked up at the ceiling, his eyes blinking fast as though he was trying to hold back tears. "My luck ran out, and if I didn't pay Malcolm back, he was going to come after you and Savannah. That is, after he took care of me."

"You borrowed money from Malcolm?"

"Yeah, a long time ago, before I knew what he was doing to you." He sniffed and finally met her gaze again. "He'd come to the club that night to find me. I've been trying to find a way to get the money. I'd have a run of good luck, only to lose everything on the next card. Then, when I was let go from the team, I ran out of options.

"The night of the gala, I came home to find him waiting for me. Said he needed the money for his medical and legal bills. But he would let it go if I told him where to find you and Savannah."

Her stomach knotted. Her lawyer, Tasha, had made sure Malcolm's bail was set so high that he wouldn't be able to post it. And yet, he had. And he was out there, somewhere, still trying to exact revenge.

"I didn't know what else to do." Tre ran his hand over his face again. "I wasn't going to let him hurt you again. Not after what he did to you before. And if I told him where you and Savannah were, who knows what he would've done to y'all."

Probably no different than what Tre was doing now. She bit back the bitter remark and nodded.

"So I showed him the checks and asked him to wait until today. I paid him the hundred grand I owed him, and the rest, I was going to take to Vegas to see if I could win some of the money back before you realized it was missing." He turned to her, his expression earnest like he believed his actions were justifiable. "I was going to pay it back, Kiana. All of it. And then some."

"Why didn't you just ask Mama for a loan?"

"I was too embarrassed. You know how she feels about gambling, and I was already too deep in the hole."

"But you know she would've helped you out. A mother's love is unconditional." Denise had shown that to her more times than she could count, and she wasn't even the woman's flesh and blood.

"No. I had a plan. And it was going to work." His voice rose in anger, and he aimed the gun at her again. "Until you decided to call the cops on me."

Her mouth grew dry, and she fought to keep her voice calm. "What makes you think it was me?"

"It had to be you. No one else would've noticed the money was missing. I was checking into my flight to Las Vegas, and they wouldn't give me my boarding pass. Oh, they tried to be discreet, but I overheard one of them calling the cops. And that's when I knew you'd turned me in. You betrayed me."

No, Tre, you betrayed me. How she wanted to say those words, but judging by how close his finger was to the trigger, it would only earn her a bullet.

The ringing of her phone shattered the silence, and both of them jumped. The first few chords of "Bad to the Bone" echoed through the condo.

Frank's ringtone. He told her that it was the ringtone his eldest brother had assigned to him, and she did the same as a joke.

Only now, it wasn't a laughing matter.

By some small miracle, Tre didn't fire the gun, but he did lower the barrel to her purse. "Don't answer."

"But it's Frank." Slowly, she pulled out the phone and showed him the screen with the caller ID. "If I don't answer, he'll know something's wrong."

Tre's body rippled like a toddler in the middle of a temper tantrum, complete with the single stomp of his foot. "Shit! Fine. Answer him, but don't tell him about me. Everything is all right here. Understood?"

He leveled the gun at her, and the consequences to her disobeying him became very clear.

She pressed the answer button and put the phone up to her ear.

"Kiana, is Tre with you?"

The urgency in his voice almost proved to be her undoing. Tears gathered in the corners of her eyes, and she covered her mouth to stifle the sob that wanted to break free. A second later, she'd gathered enough composure to say, "Yes, Frank?"

She made her voice rise at the end so Tre would think she was answering the call rather than Frank's question.

Frank swore. "Are you safe?"

"I'm sorry, Frank, but no." She glanced over at Tre to see if he was falling for her act. "Tonight's not a good night."

More swearing. "I'm coming up."

"No, please, don't. I'm exhausted."

A gap of silence followed, and she pictured Frank putting the pieces together. "Holy shit, Kiana, does he have a gun?"

"Absolutely." She stared at the barrel and added, "Maybe we can get together for dinner later this week."

Tre rolled his eyes and gestured for her to hurry up.

Some of the dread choking her throat eased up. At least her brother had no clue what was really being said.

"Agent Phillips is on his way. Get some place safe if you can. Savannah, too."

"Of course." She glanced one more time at Tre. "I have to go. Savannah needs me, but—" Her voice caught, and a new fear surfaced. There was a chance she might not talk to Frank ever again, and she needed to tell him how she felt while she still could. "I love you."

She hung up before an awkward pause followed. She wanted to believe he loved her, too. It was better to cling to that hope than to be handed the contrary truth.

"What did Frank want?" Tre asked.

"He wanted to take me and Savannah out to dinner." A lie, but one Tre had to believe if she wanted to get out of this alive. "I convinced him that tonight wasn't going to work."

"Smart girl. Now, turn your phone off and hand it to me."

She did as she was told and waited for his next instructions. If she could just keep him talking until the FBI arrived, then maybe—just maybe—she would live to see the sunrise.

***

Frank stared out into nothing as the cold hum of a dial

199

tone filled his ears. A second before, Kiana's voice had filled the line. She was alive, but in danger. But that was nothing compared to the last three words he'd heard from her.

She loved him.

Something squeezed around his chest when he heard her tell him that. It pressed the air from his lungs and left his head swimming.

Kiana loved him, and he knew in that instant that he loved her back.

Only she'd robbed him of the chance of telling her so by hanging up.

He found Agent Phillips's number and called him back. "Get up here now. Tre's in her place, and he has a gun."

"Got it," Phillips replied without an ounce of urgency. "We'll keep that in mind."

The agent hung up, and Frank was left standing in front of the locked door that mocked him from the parking garage. There had to be another way to get into the building. Then he remembered the security guard in the lobby and ran for the front door.

As he made his way through the parking garage to the street, he replayed his conversation with Kiana. She'd been smart to talk in code, to answer his questions but make it sound like something else. It told her that Tre was in the same room with her and he was listening.

A new wave of fear washed over him and quickened his steps. He had to save her. He had to tell her how he felt about her, about Savannah, about everything. But if he waited for the FBI to arrive, it might be too late. And if Tre had been tipped off for any reason...

That thought slowed his steps as he approached the lobby of Kiana's building. He forced himself to walk calmly into the building as he had over the weekend with Kiana and Savannah. He waved to the security guard.

Luckily, the same guard was on duty and waved back at him.

First hurdle cleared. Now to the next one.

He tried to remember the code Kiana had entered for the elevator and got it on the second try. The elevator inside didn't have buttons. It automatically took the occupants to the floors that corresponded to the codes entered. When it stopped on her floor, Frank hesitated.

This wasn't like the night in the club where he'd acted on instinct and swung blindly. This time, he knew the people inside. He cared about them. And he knew the stakes involved. One misstep, and someone could end up dead.

He considered waiting for the FBI to arrive, but as the doors started to close, he jutted his hand out to stop them.

Negotiation. That was what this called for. Not an ambush.

He stepped out of the elevator and wiped his hands on his jeans. What he wouldn't give to have Ben or Dan by his side. His two older brothers had always been the peacekeepers among them. Ben was the brute, and Dan was the brains. Together, they could always break things up when things got heated or came to blows.

He pressed his ear against the cold steel of Kiana's door and listened.

Muffled voices came from the other side. He couldn't understand them, but it told him enough. Kiana was on the other side, and Tre likely was, too.

A split second later, he found himself hoping Savannah wasn't in the room. He'd only just met Kiana's little girl, and he was already worried about her like she was his own kid.

Shit, I'm in deep.

But if he could get the two women he loved out of this, he wouldn't waste any time letting them know how precious they were to him.

Tre's voice grew louder, and Kiana yelped. It was all he needed to hear. She was in danger, and he needed to act now.

He entered her key code and rammed the door open.

Everything around him seemed to move in slow motion.

Tre stood a dozen feet away with a gun pointed at Kiana, who was standing in the kitchen.

He turned to face Frank.

Frank lowered his hand and rushed him.

A gunshot rang through the room, followed by the sound of shattering glass. A woman's scream followed.

It was the club all over again.

Only this time, Kiana wasn't there to deflect the shots.

Another shot rang out, and a line of fire tore across his upper arm.

It threw him just enough off balance so he didn't hit Tre in the center of his gut like he'd been coached to do by countless linebacker coaches. Instead, he caught Tre's arm. He twisted his weight and held on tight, bringing Tre down with him.

They rolled to the ground, but Frank used his size to

his advantage and pinned Tre beneath him.

A faint ding from the elevator down the hall caught his attention, but he refused to let it distract him from the man in front of him.

A twinge of regret pierced his chest as he punched his friend's face.

Next, he grabbed Tre's gun arm and twisted.

A snap of bone vibrated through his hands.

The gun clattered to the floor.

Frank stared into the wide eyes of his friend and swung.

"Stop!"

At the sound of Kiana's voice, he froze, his fist inches from Tre's face.

Footsteps pounded behind him, but he only cared about one person in the room.

Kiana stood in the kitchen, tears streaming down her cheeks. She stretched her hands out in front of her. "Everyone, please, just stop."

Frank relaxed and lowered his fists.

A pair of agents pried him off of Tre and swooped in to make an arrest, but he never took his eyes off of her.

She was alive, and that was all that mattered to him.

The FBI agents dragged Tre toward the door, clearing the space between Frank and Kiana.

He ran to her and pulled her into his arms. "Where's Savannah?"

"In her room with Madison."

"Thank God." He hugged Kiana so tightly, he worried he might crush her. She was soft and warm and so very alive.

"Frank, you're hurt." She pushed him away and pointed to the growing red stain on the sleeve of his shirt. "We need to get you to the ER."

"I'm fine." He wiped away the tears on her cheek.

"No, you are getting checked out, and don't you dare try to argue with me." She lifted her chin in that stubborn little way of hers, and he couldn't help but smile.

"Do you have any idea how much I love you?"

A hesitant smile formed on her lips. "You love me?"

"Would I risk my life to save you and your little girl if I didn't?"

Her smile widened, and she made a sound that was a mixture of a laugh and a sob. "I don't know, Romeo. I've heard about your reputation for starting fights," she teased.

"Just shut up and kiss me before I throw you over my shoulder and take you to bed."

She laughed even as the tears continued to roll down her cheeks. "Gladly."

Their lips had barely met before Agent Phillips cleared his throat behind them. "I'm going to need statements from both of you, preferably before the medics get here."

A warm trickle flowed down his arm, and his bicep started to throb as the adrenaline waned. He was about ready for those medics and their pain meds. "Sure thing, Agent Phillips."

"Just let me check on my daughter." Kiana dashed toward the back of the condo.

Agent Phillips trailed after her. "There were other hostages?"

Savannah's prattle filtered in from down the hall, and

his last fears ebbed. Both of his girls were safe.

And once this was all behind them, he was going to make sure they knew how much they meant to him.

CHAPTER EIGHTEEN

Kiana smoothed the wrinkles out of her crisp cotton dress as Frank pulled into the winery in Woodinville, Washington. The July sun beat down on them through the car windows, so contrary to the rainy weather she'd always associated with Seattle. "Do I look okay?"

"Honey, you're always lovely, no matter what you're wearing." Of course, the heat in his eyes told her he found her most lovely wearing nothing at all.

"But I want to make a good first impression." They were here for the wedding of his older brother, Dan. She got out of the car and opened the back door to get Savannah, only to find Frank had beat her to it. "This is the first time I'm meeting your family, after all."

"And I keep telling you, they'll adore both my lovely ladies." He tickled Savannah as he released her from the car seat. "Isn't that right, Sugar Pie?"

Savannah wrinkled her nose with a grin at the sound of Frank's nickname for her and reached for something inside his jacket. "Pretty."

"Yes, you are." He guided her hand away.

"No! Pretty!" Savannah pawed at his jacket again. "Now."

Kiana rushed to them and took her daughter before the two-year-old burst into a full-out temper tantrum. "Any idea what she wants?"

Frank gave her a sheepish grin and scratched the back of his head. "Well, I was going to save this for after the wedding, but..."

"But what?"

"Pretty!" Savannah insisted and reached for his inside jacket pocket again.

Frank pulled out a small velvet-covered box and handed it to her. "Okay, I guess we can give it to your mama now."

Savannah grinned and passed the box to Kiana.

"What is this?" she asked, not sure if she was ready for what could be inside.

"Something Savannah helped me pick out." He crossed his arms and tried to look smug, but the pink tips of his ears revealed his uncertainty. "Open it."

She set Savannah down, her gaze never leaving the small square box. Her hands shook as she opened it. Nestled inside was the most perfect diamond solitaire ring she'd ever seen. Her breath hitched. "Frank!"

When her gaze shifted from the ring to him, she found him kneeling on the ground, hugging Savannah. "I already have her permission. What do you say to having one of these wedding things for ourselves in a few months?"

Her eyes stung with unshed tears, and her voice choked on the flood of emotions rolling through her. "Are you asking me to marry you?"

"No, I'm asking you to plan a wedding for me," he teased. "Of course, you'd have to be the bride, and I'll be the groom, and Savannah can give you away."

A twinge of regret coursed through her. Her father was gone. Tre was in jail for embezzling funds from the foundation, shooting Frank, and holding her hostage. But she already knew Denise adored Frank and would walk her down the aisle. "You've thought this all out, huh?"

He rose and pulled her into his arms. "I've been thinking about it for months. The hardest part was convincing your daughter that I'd be good to you."

"You always have been." She pressed her forehead against his. "And yes, I'll marry you."

"That makes me the luckiest guy in the world."

His lips brushed against hers in a tender kiss that was interrupted by a pat on her leg and a small voice going, "Pretty."

Kiana laughed and took the ring from the box. "I'd better put this on before Savannah tries to steal it for herself."

"Like I said, she helped me pick it out." Frank took the ring and slipped it on her left ring finger. "Beautiful, just like my two girls."

Kiana looked into his eyes and knew she'd found the man she'd been waiting for. He loved her and her daughter. He made her feel safe. And he made her heart sing with every glance, every touch, every soft-spoken word. "I love you."

"I love you, too." He grinned and reached for Savannah. "And you too, Sugar Pie."

Savannah giggled and ran out of his grasp, looking back over her shoulder the whole time. She never saw the stately woman with silver hair in front of her.

Kiana's cheeks burned when her daughter collided with the woman, and she rushed forward to help Savannah up. "I'm so sorry about that," she said to the woman.

"It's quite all right," she replied, picking Savannah up into her arms. The toddler grew quiet, studying the older woman with a serious expression. "And who is this lovely lady, Frank?"

"That is Savannah, Mom."

A new wave of embarrassment washed over her. Savannah had practically knocked her future grandmother off her feet. "I can take her from you."

"Nonsense." Frank's mom rubbed noses with Savannah. "I've heard so much about the both of you, and now that I have a little girl to spoil, I'm not going to let her go."

Savannah grinned back at her like she understood exactly what lay in store for her.

Frank's mom tore her attention away from Savannah. "I'm Maureen, Frank's mother. It's so nice to finally meet you, Kiana."

"The same goes for me."

"If you have Savannah, Mom, I'm going to escort Kiana to her seat." Frank tucked her left hand into the crook of his arm, and the sunlight caught on the diamond.

Maureen's eyes widened, as did her smile. "Is that what I think it is?"

Frank held his finger to his lips. "Shh! This is Dan and Jenny's day."

His mom squealed and bounced Savannah in her arms. "Let me be the first to offer my congratulations." Then she turned her attention back to the toddler in her arms. "And you can start calling me 'Grandma.'"

Savannah blew her raspberry, earning another delightful laugh from Maureen.

"She is just a doll, Kiana." Frank's mom hugged Savannah and started walking toward the rows of chairs set up behind the winery. "I'm going to have so much fun spoiling you."

Frank winked at her. "See? I come by it naturally."

"I always knew you were something else, Frank Kelly."

"And I always knew you were the girl for me." He covered his hand with his own and placed a kiss on her cheek. "Ready to meet the rest of the family?"

She paused and ran her free hand over her dress one more time, only to have Frank stop her and tilt her chin up to face him.

"I'm right here beside you until the very end," he said with a soft sincerity that filled her with a warm glow.

The last of her fears vanished, and she smiled up at the one man she wanted to spend the rest of her life with. "Same here, Romeo."

A Note to Readers

Dear Reader,

Thank you so much for reading *In the Red Zone*. I hope you enjoyed it and look forward to the final book in the series, *Here All Along*. If you did, please leave a review at the store where you bought this book or on Goodreads.

I love to hear from readers. You can find me on Facebook and Twitter, or you can email me using the contact form on my website, www.CristaMcHugh.com.

If you would like to be the first to know about new releases or be entered into exclusive contests, please sign up for my newsletter using the contact form on my website at http://bit.ly/19EJAW8.

Also, please like my Facebook page for more excerpts and teasers from upcoming books. And, just for this series, I have a special website featuring more information on the Kelly Brothers, playlists, recipes, and other extras just for readers. Please check it out at www.thekellybrothers.cristamchugh.com.

--*Crista*

Don't miss the final book in the Kelly Brothers series...

HERE ALL ALONG

THE KELLY BROTHERS, BOOK 7

Can close friends have a romance worthy of a Hollywood love story?

Coming in August 2015...

Sign up for Crista's Newsletter to be the first to know when *Here All Along* is available.

Author Bio

Growing up in small town Alabama, Crista relied on storytelling as a natural way for her to pass the time and keep her two younger sisters entertained.

She currently lives in the Audi-filled suburbs of Seattle with her husband and two children, maintaining her alter ego of mild-mannered physician by day while she continues to pursue writing on nights and weekends.

Just for laughs, here are some of the jobs she's had in the past to pay the bills: barista, bartender, sommelier, stagehand, actress, morgue attendant, and autopsy assistant.

And she's also a recovering LARPer. (She blames it on her crazy college days)

For the latest updates, deleted scenes, and answers to any burning questions you have, please check out her webpage, www.CristaMcHugh.com.

Sign up for Crista's 99c New Release Newsletter at http://bit.ly/19EJAW8

Find Crista online at:

Twitter: twitter.com/crista_mchugh

Facebook: www.facebook.com/CristaMcHugh

CPSIA information can be obtained at www.ICGtesting.com
Printed in the USA
LVOW11s1036250515

439709LV00007BA/627/P